CW00924106

KNOCK TURN

A NOVEL BY JEB LOY NICHOLS

PUSHCART PRESS
WAINSCOTT, NEW YORK

Illustrations by Jeb Loy Nichols
Designed by Mary Kornblum

ISBN 979-8-9854697-0-7

Published by Pushcart Press
P.O. Box 380 Wainscott, NY 11975

Distributed by WW Norton & Company, Inc
500 Fifth Avenue New York, NY 10110

FIRST EDITION

For Loraine who started it

and Thayer, Mary and Bill who finished it

They are not pictures.
They are a place.
• MARK ROTHKO

Most reckless things
are beautiful in some way.
• JOHN ASHBERRY

What planet is this?
Is this a planet of life or death?
• SUN RA

A roomful of portraits by William Roberts. Dark browns, mud, umbers, flinty greys. A red scarf, a wedge of blue. A line of raspberry jam. Mostly I remember his wife Sarah, posed rigid by a window, holding a letter, playing a bamboo flute. His son too, during the war. And a slew of self portraits. Two rooms, forty canvases. Fifty years through which I tip-toed. Who, these days, remembers William Roberts? The Vorticist. The man about whom the New York Times, in 1931, said, "He finds the essential simplicities behind the masquerade of convention...these brilliantly transformed men and women; gesture, pose, grimace, seem more real than the original reality." The man who, when asked if he ever got bored painting Sarah, year after year, said: the great adventure is to see something unknown appear each day in the same face.

They, the nonrememberers, speak firmly. Rarely do they equivocate. They know who they are. They are, increasingly, incredible, unblemished. They are not their parent's children. They have no need of either the Vorticists or William Roberts.

My father knew William Roberts. They stood shoulder to shoulder in womanless photos. They exchanged letters, invitations, postcards. They wore the same grey suits, the same shapeless hats. They both had little hair. Neither was particularly, as concerns the world of fame and commerce, ambitious. They both, most days, applied paint to canvas. The portraits I'm remembering now, of Roberts' wife and family, I saw twenty years ago at the National Portrait Gallery, fifteen years after my father's death. Day after day I went, silently circling the room, deliberating, looking into those dark, flat eyes, remembering how to remember.

Here we come, we two, on a narrow boat, slowly, from the south. Slower even than is usual, barely a ripple. The first week of September. The first week of the ninth month of the final year of the millennium. In four months it'll be a new decade, a new century, a new world in which to feel old. The cress choked water is neither green nor blue nor black nor brown; it plops and bubbles. We're heading, I suppose, roughly west, into the dim future. Moor and dingle, stile and gate, hill and valley.

What do we have for lunch?

She tells me nothing. Nudging the rudder to the left.

Quiet here.

She nods.

I slope into her hip and shoulder. The length of her. Three weeks ago, the week before we left, my doctor asked me if I knew the word kopophobia. My head shook. The fear of fatigue, my doctor said. In his off-white over-lit office; west and north and near a wooded park; no paintings on the wall, only a framed medical school diploma; a stark and unforgiving place. No music entered there.

I'm fine, I tell her. I'm good.

I try to look healthy. Younger, surer, full and fit.

Look at me, I tell her, in all this fresh air.

My doctor, both an acquaintance and a burden, two years older and more energetic, more engaged, more flexible, with better skin and stylish clothes, yoga every morning and sailing on the weekends, smiled and said, what will be will be.

He's had, over the years, a series of athletic affairs, often with his nurses.

On the side of the canal yellow flowers flap. Poppies perhaps or buttercups. Swiveling sticks and leaves. Crisp wrappers too and plastic bags. Red and white amongst the green. The footpaths where come solitary men and women with their dogs. She pushes gently at the rudder and reaches for the radio.

Do you mind?

I move my lips but don't speak. A click, some static, and a tiny, hushed voice joins us on the boat, talking earnestly about Chopin, Schubert, Peter Warlock. The lunchtime concert, one o'clock. There's muted applause and a piano begins its tinkle, tinkle. Then silence. Then mumble. Then tinkle. Then more and more tinkling. Slowly on and on. It means little to me, it occupies space in the air, it fills time, it dallies and then, in a blink, disappears. Nothing specific lingers. I lean in the stillness and am blank.

We had, once, cycled across the river to be amongst the clappers. The well meaning attenders of such events. Those with a mid-day hour to spare.

In large coats that flapped around our knees. The bikes we rode were old, of the kind now rarely seen, black beauties that weighed a ton, with wicker baskets on the front. We each listened in our own distinct way; she familiar, focused, me drifting.

We'd come from Camberwell, from a tiny flat on a street that housed a hundred others just like it. A flat in which we lived thirty years. A flat owned and maintained by the local council. Where, during the day, she taught an uneven parade of hopefuls how to play cello.

The years, I don't know, uneasily perhaps, obscured somehow, were barely lived, until a whole heap had vanished.

Still the piano tinkles.

I ask her: where exactly are we, and she, whispering, says, I've no idea.

There is, around these parts, these hills and highlands, a great lessening and depletion of field birds. Pheasants and such like. A sixty per cent drop over the past ten years. I've read the reports, collected articles.

Wave bye-bye to the Red Legged Partridge. Also the Curlew. Also the Meadow Pipit. Also the Green Plover. Also the Lapwing and Peewit. Also the Hedge Sparrow.

There is also, around these parts, an ever decreasing human population. Human *presence*, however, has never been more evident. Everywhere you look you see the signs: domesticated farm animals, pesticides, the introduction of non-native trees and plants, the draining of marsh lands, intensive farming, the destruction of natural habitats, the prettifying of open spaces.

Roads too and miles of barb wire fencing. The roar of quad bikes. Also quarries and vast, ugly, metal barns.

If you've never heard the song of the Linnet, chances are you never will.

I grew up here with my father. In these hills. In these hills that had raised him and his father before him. He had gone, when he was twenty, for six overwhelming months, to London. He returned and never again left. I too went to London when I was twenty. I stayed for thirty years, doing nothing of any great importance; I'm now, I suppose, in the process of returning. The neighbourhood had become over full and always loud; the hecticness unbearable. The shouting and the motors and all the cramped bits that never lulled. The diesel hum and the leaf blowers. The radio's thump. On and on it stretched, for miles in every direction. Only increasing; never did it grow smaller, or quieter, or less ugly. It first wearied then claimed me, replicating, in my organs, the various turmoils of the city. My body, internally, began to bleed. I found myself out of breath, without energy. I submitted to tests; I was prodded and left sitting in empty hallways. Stress, the doctor finally said. A rare kind of stomach ulcer. Related to peptic ulcers but less directly treatable. My blood, he said, wasn't strong enough to cure it. It wasn't carrying the correct antibodies. I denied them their antibiotics and blue pills. I went it alone. In my own way. A combined regime of leafy foods, long walks, meditation and grudging acceptance. Great big dumb mistake, my friend the doctor said sadly. Speaking as a man with experience in these matters.

In his room without air, without tenderness.

That was one year ago.

She was, when we met, much freckled, a face mottled and sprayed. I approached her slowly, being twenty-one and permanently nervous. I hoped I might learn to play the cello. It was a thought I had. Something about the way Pablo Casals leant over his instrument. The curve of his shoulder. The connection he made with an unhuman partner. For three months I wasted her time. Practiced and made no progress. I fooled no one. My shoulder, the curve of my back, my rigid fingers, all wrong. Without grace, without melody. In desperation I took her to dinner. We discussed French thinkers and the situation in Cuba. We heaped scorn on pet owners, on monarchists, on the clergy, on anyone who wore velvet. We were, in a slight way, serious. We skipped dessert. She let it be known that I would never be a musician. We walked home slowly, through the worst bits of Forest Hill. Saying almost nothing. We repeated the entire scenario frequently throughout the summer. Then, according to the fashion of those days, we married. She called me Mouse, as in shy, skittish, as in frightened of bright lights.

I had a job selling books. The shop's specialty was French and European translations; also, in the back room, shelves of science fiction. The clientele never mixed. The musty academics over there, muttering, close to the counter; the graceless teens in back. Men and women out of step with the brightness of the times. We sold a few translated volumes each week; we sold bags of science fiction. We eked out a living. We kept the lights dim. Never did I dust nor apply fresh paint. I sat amongst Asimov and Foucault and Pavese and waited. An apt word: eke. An exclamation signifying a fear of the world. What people say when they see a mouse.

Mouse, she used to say, you gotta relax. Then, when least expected, shout, BANG! Causing my heart to flutter. That's the way it was with her, first one thing and then another.

That's the way it still is. First this then that.

Like this, listening to these French fellas with their complicated tinkling. She's got her eyes closed and it's like she's in a spell. All mesmerised. Still freckled and still sprayed; tempting still, her hair grey now but great to look at. I'd rather watch her than anything. Her lips and eyes and the way she sits so still while we do our watery creep. Giving nothing away. I think I'm familiar but who really knows what goes on? Who can say? Not me. I assume nothing. She's a surpriser.

My father too, though severe in his ways, was a confounder. His paintings, in several important museums, are no longer shown. It seems they've fallen from favour. Times having moved on. I've been approached by collectors, by connoisseurs. I've had official letters, been visited by the heads of provincial art departments. I tell them all: I barely knew him. I know even less about his paintings. I have three that he gave me. The others have vanished into private collections, into small museums, into dim vaults.

I think of his turpentined hands, his blackened nails, the smell and stroll of him. Thin and rabbitish; chew, sniff, flinch, tremble. His eyes aquiver. No part of him at rest.

I remember him bending over me at my desk. *My* desk in *my* room, picking up the book *I* was reading. Raising his eyebrows and, smiling, meaning no harm, saying, trash.

To which I was silent. I didn't nod, I didn't smile, I didn't turn. I'd learnt my lessons well. He returned the book and skittered away.

Trash perhaps. A small, bright paperback that cost almost nothing. Space travel, strange dwellers on distant shores, weaponry made of hardened light. Airmen and treacherous women. On the cover a many armed, scaled beast.

I was old enough to suspect that the world, the whole world, was awash with trash. Absolutely swimming in it. That the world of men and women, the world of shops and school and church and transport was *in fact* trash. Trash being our building blocks, our life blood. Trash being what we made, what we talked, what we moved from place to place. What we wore, what we believed, what we loved and worshiped. What we were.

It's true that 90 per cent of science fiction is rubbish, but then 90 per cent of everything is rubbish.

So said Theodore Sturgeon.

The tinkling comes to an end, finished by a murmur of applause. She opens her eyes, clicks off the radio; we drift.

Most of everything I've left behind. My precious piles and heaps, my trappings. Books and records and dumb little collected scraps of paper. Thirty years of waking. Can't have it here. No room. I feel both less weighty and stripped. I am deleafed, bare. There was a box I had, an old shoe box, upon which it said Jones of Mayfair, that was full of pencils. That I miss. Mostly unsharpened. Given away at various events. The name of a business or some such thing printed on them. I liked the look and size of them; collected in book fairs, at publishers; back when I moved about in the world, buying books.

Back when I had opinions.

When I was a very different kettle of fish.

Such as what are swimming below us now.

If indeed these waterways include fish; I've seen only weeds, plastic bottles and bags. Bugs skimming on the surface. Ducks too and geese. Perhaps the deeper water is too toxified, too leaden, too long among humans.

Her forehead, the corners of her eyes, her hands are barely marked. Hair, at her neck, aswish. Four years older than me but uncreased. I've often thought of her as an unhuman human, a visitor. A singular being. Of the kind that populated the books my father dismissed as trash. That I later sold by the bag full. I've met no other of her tribe. Her home not here but elsewhere. Not amongst these hardened soldiers. These copiers and dimwits. These dullards.

Swish and giggle goes the water; hungry? asks Bev.

I could eat.

She nods.

I stand, slowly, and make my way to the cabin door. In the cabin, on the table, is the book she's reading. The Sane Society by Eric Fromm. Also: her cello in a black case, a box of food, a soft bag of clothes, a wicker picnic basket. I grab the picnic basket and return.

They played the nocturne too fast. She says.

The tendency being, in all things, to rush.

The first section, she says, should crawl.

She talks quietly, watching the canal sides.

And why, she asks, when they go to the A minor, must they use vibrato?

The tendency being, these days, to flutter. To pulse. To be always, even slightly, moving.

2

The sole cause of man's unhappiness is that he does not know how to stay quietly in his room.

So wrote Blaise Pascal.

L ook at my father in his hey day. In his grey tweed suit, his thick soled shoes, his lingering pipe, his beret. Standing at his easel, palette board aloft, staring at the arrangement in front of him. Commanding, among his peers, a certain respect. He was one of them, he was neither more nor less. His compatriots grunted approval. Where William Roberts gaze fell mainly on people, my father focused on household objects. Arrangements of scissors and tea cups, wine bottles and milk jugs, a ball of twine, a hair brush. Look, there at the table: a bowl, two mugs, a vase. A box of matches. Over and over again, with slight variations. The same objects in different light. One jar replaced with another. One colour more pale.

His exhibitions were well received. His paintings sold. They disappeared into the world. One was bought by Roger Fry. Another by Leonard Woolf. The Tate bought a small painting of a dinner plate and a serving spoon. Also one of a salt cellar and a basket. Each year he sent something to the Royal

Academy. And yet never was he in the first rank, never was he, away from his colleagues, a talking point. He painted and he sold; it was what he did. Never was he celebrated. Each day he went to the studio at the end of the garden. Piled high with canvases and oil paints. A fire hazard. Mouse riddled. Selling just enough to keep us in our reduced circumstances. Accustomed as we were to life in the Welsh hills, a life without Spain, without pudding, without pets, without cars, without tennis, without the beach. Without those things often enjoyed by our neighbours. Which kept us separate and worrisome. Suspects. We were, in the neighbourhood, not trusted.

Shall I cook something?

Bev nods and I walk back to the cabin. I open a small fridge and take out an onion, an apple, a chilli, some ginger, a red pepper, a block of tofu. Some chopping is involved. I turn on the gas ring and find a pan. Some oil is involved, sesame seeds and cumin. As I fry I whistle the theme from Robin Hood. Neither well nor loudly. Mostly to myself. The William Tell thing. Dum diddy dum, diddy dum dum dum. Whilst whistling I remember my father's habit of boiling three eggs each morning to take to the studio.

The studio; a becalmed, unweathered place. Outside time, history, outside the cheap give and take of commerce.

In the morning kitchen, over toast and tea

and marmalade, we were companionable. Two Welshmen of the Montgomeryshire region, me in my school uniform, he besuited. I enjoyed being with him. He treated me as he treated all his friends; with caution, softly, always on the alert, without a hint of either irony or scorn. While I readied myself for school, he prepared for the studio.

The kitchen was as his mother had left it, fifteen years previous. Nothing out of place, scented still, all tidy, scrubbed. Tea towelled and serene. Ghostly, to be honest. My father being a firm believer in soap and order. Also in silence, in brevity, in less, in Cezzane, in Piero Di Cosimo. In soda crystals and scouring pads. In Bach and Vivaldi. I believe this, he once told me: people speak too loudly and at too great a length about too little.

We eat dinner silently. Plates on our laps, on the narrow benches near the rudder. The engine off, stationary almost. A slow dusk. We light two citronella candles to keep off the midges. I wonder what they want with an old man's weak blood. Surely, by now, it's stale, poisonous, past its sale by date. There must be, locally, better targets then me. Get away, I whisper to them, go find some young flesh for your dinner. Later I gather the plates, lean over the side and swish them in water.

Bev is readying her cello, tightening the bow, tuning up. Her nightly hour. My favourite hour. She plays what she plays and I listen. In a wandering way, not attentively. My gambolling thoughts. I suppose the pieces she plays have names; nocturnes and preludes and sonatas, composers too, who somehow wove this lace of notes, but I don't ask. I let them be what they are without names. I sit and it's kind of perfect. A blanket over my legs, stars and moon above, planes and satellites too, too far away to be oppressive, bats in the trees, water below, a murmur of movement, the measured sound of the cello.

The word they used, the nurses and the doctors, about my ulcers, was *irregular*, a word I approved of, a word I often apply to myself. Everything about me is irregular, why not my stomach? This isn't, they said, any kind of cancer, rather a tear in my stomach lining that refuses to heal. It was something to do with my blood being less than vigorous. It sulked around. No longer did it rush hither and thither; where once it hastened now it moped. The fact being that all things slow, all things lessen. My stomach, I told them, is mine, and I will deal with it.

Bev's playing something familiar. I should know what it is. I should have, these past forty years, paid more attention. The notes are long and low and then, unexpectedly, higher and faster. French, I think. The music, like the bats, darts around. It will, before it ends, get very quiet. They all do, the pieces she plays. Bev's fingers do something complicated, something beyond my seeing, producing a swooshing effect, and I wish she wouldn't stop.

Something, perhaps a newt, makes a small splash. I have no clear idea of what a newt looks like. Nor why the word newt has suddenly popped into my mind. Perhaps something I've read. I'm picturing something that's half frog, half fish. Tail like a fin and tiny webbed feet. Striped, like a lizard. Three inches long. I'm wondering what kind of life a newt has. If it has a family or a mate, how it survives the winter, how it spends the hours between sundown and midnight. Thinking of a newspaper article I read that said around half of all amphibian species are in decline; a third are threatened with extinction. At which point, for some reason, I remember my first encounter with Miles Davis. A record borrowed from a friend. Miles in his mid cool period. Sharkskin suit and thin tie. Muted and measured; there was an anger, a brittleness, a low lidded reservoir of wariness. My father sat with me and listened. This was something brand new for us both. We played the first side and then, after a moment, the second. Neither of us spoke. He took it, and me, seriously. When it ended he nodded once, whispered well well, and stood. Standing as he often stood, puzzled, belated; a man not at the centre of his own life. Looking around the room as if uncertain how he came to be there.

During the last ten years of his life, when I was home on a visit, I often found him in his dimmed studio, staring at some arrangement, listening to Kind Of Blue. In front of him three plates, a candle, a colander; around him more canvases and mice, cold cups of tea, beveled bottles of turpentine.

Bev, unlit and nearly unseeable, continues her obligatos and crescendos. She used to, in our Camberwell flat, practice in the morning after breakfast. After marmalade and toast and lemony tea. In the back room, overlooking our patio garden. (Our pots of calendula and Spanish sage, pots of rosemary and lavender.) I like this better. Out in the open darkened quiet. She and her cello, me and my weak blood. Above us the not weak bats. With the not weak bugs and tiny birds. The whole vast not weak starriness. Untrod upon and always. Stars and what have you. The thing I mostly feel now is not weak exactly but cut off, disentangled from London and what I was there. Unloosened. The yodelling streets and neoned corners. The drunks and loopy dogs. Drifts of grease stained rubbish. My familiar supports vamoosed.

London, London
dog eyed whore
I'll roam and rove
and return no more
So said the words of an 18th century sea shanty.

London had become indefensible. A kennel of rich

dullards. All that was stealable was stolen; all that was sellable was sold. There were only, at all times, cheap and chronic negotiations. Up and down they paraded, these fresh citizens, these oligarchs, these nonrememberers. These land grabbers. The stink of good fortune on them. With their tight trousers and thin hips. I watched them from my burrow, mystified. Who were they? From whence had they come? What language did they speak? I wished them ill, all of them, I was bad minded; I invented tortures and knifings. I wished catastrophes for their loved ones, floods for their homes, weakened bones and poison for their pets. I didn't enjoy thinking this way. I realised that, as long as I remained amongst them, I would be an anachronism, a malingerer. I would also be no good to myself.

The things I loved were no longer of value. They were muck. I had become an irrelevance in my own neighbourhood. I was no longer needed. I was old and therefore worthless. I took comfort in sickness. Also solitariness. Also forgetfulness. Large hats and comfortable shoes. The sugary food of my youth. Whole sections of my life slipped away. Names, towns, travels, loves, cars, friends. All forgotten.

I looked with sadness upon children, an entire generation, who would not be allowed to forget. The internet, this monstrous presence, this flesh eating disease, would record and make available every childhood friend, every family function, every hair style, every tedious event in their over documented lives.

Well, well, said I on my shambling walks, you dumb little shits. You acquisitors. You can have it. It's yours. The neighbourhood, the night, the city, the electricity, the sewers, the buses, the chicken wraps, the once dirty parks, the shops, the sales, the dull scramble it's become.

The choice was clear: stay and be dead or leave and live.

I wrote the two options on a piece of paper. LIFE / DEATH. I sat and deliberated. Leaning first this way and then that. Believing, briefly, in myself. In my untidy shop amongst the longhaired and the bald. With one flickering light and the windows smeary. I made lists. I was methodical. On the one hand was oblivion, release, non-involvement, sleep eternal, full stop. On the other hand were mushrooms, autumn, jazz, lavender, clean bedding, Bev. It came down, I felt, to water versus sand. I made no definite decision.

My father died at sixty-one; last month I turned seventy. Hooray for lucky me.

And this: all the loving I've done, of my father, of Bev, of jazz, of books, has helped me not one jot. Brought no lasting wisdom, comfort, relief. It's simply filled time. For which I'm grateful. I continue to be frightened and bored, often anxious, lonely and, when least expected, amused. I have tried to be equable and failed. It's made me neither a better man nor happier. I am who I am.

Bev zips her cello into its padded case. Something's humming, maybe Bev or the lapping water or maybe the birch leaves. A little, thin, sand papery noise. Not exactly a tune, more like a tune before it's a tune. On its way to becoming. Bev joins me on the bench and we say nothing, just sit surrounded and out numbered by the night. Her hand finds mine. There's some squeezing and some patting. Our fingers fit together. It's a little bit chilly and I could use a jacket over my jumper. Above us stuff is happening. A lot of stuff. Below us too and left and right. Happening and not happening, seen and unseen. Things for which there are no words. Things that cause me, slightly, to feel foreign. As I hunker down into my jumper Bev leans in close and whispers, have you ever noticed that there's so much of everything?

3

*We who are born into this age of freedom
and independence and the self must undergo
this loneliness. It's the price we pay
for these times of ours.*

So wrote Natsume Soseki.

Never a musician nor writer nor painter nor businessman, nor teacher nor clergy, nor thief nor bus conductor, nothing titled, nothing purposeful; who and what was I? I sputtered. Never dramatically, a tiny pop and gurgle. I made little impression on the world. Hiding there in the basement gloom of McPherson's Second Hand Books. Five years after I started there McPherson moved back to Dublin; I kept the shop. Have it son, it's yours, McPherson said. Better you than me.

The shop was rented from a man named Ric. No K. A man who slow motioned around the neighbourhood, collecting money in unmarked envelopes. He smelled raw. He was of the type that was always in the midst of something else; deals, conversations, affairs, styles, meals. He owned the building and others like it. He maintained a flat upstairs that he rarely used. He was a man of whom you might say: here is someone who is not yet fossilized. Alive and without security. He was a walking entertainment.

The winds of time blew through me, leaving barely a sign of their passing, as did fads and trends and fashions, memories too and desire. News, opinions, history.

My little mouse, Bev called me.

As she calls me still.

Bev and my father, perhaps jazz and the science fiction of my youth, being the only things to have left their marks.

Which, of course, is nonsense. All and everything must, in some way, do its damage. The city, my unease there, my bicycle, Italian food, dogs, darkness, childhood pals, Southwark bridge, Celia Johnson, Dairy Milk, the IRA, mushy peas, Beckenham Woods, Snow White; all of it tattooed somewhere, however faintly.

I suppose.

Or not.

Believe me when I say I remember so little. My entire adult life spent in a book shop I can barely recall. Yes there were two rooms, a rear and a front, it was murky, it smelled strongly of mildew, it was, I think, once painted blue. There were chairs, three, around a table. A rug that, sometime in the late 80s, took on a soiled life of its own and had to be removed. A half window looked onto the pavement. The stairs moaned and whimpered.

What did I do all day?

A few sales, a few mumbled greetings. The chair in which I sat was McPherson's wing back Parker Knowles in a once floral, now faded, cover. No cash register, only a wooden box stuffed with change.

Who was I to run a book shop? Mostly I spent my days listening to records. On the same Garrard dansette that had once been in my father's studio. When he upgraded to a radiogram I rescued it; now it pumped out Coltrane and Albert Ayler, Clifford Brown and Archie Shepp, Bill Evans and Sonny Rollins.

Not one among my customers commented on the music; the academics sniffed, the teenagers suffered. I alone made arcane and thrilling connections. I alone was spellbound. I, alone. Wearing, as I often did, a dark beret. Also a beard that turned grey early. Flannel trousers and plimsoles. Jumpers of a uniform ordinariness. Owning neither a suit nor tie. Nor impressive brogues or briefcase.

I don't think I minded my burrow; I passed time without feeling damaged.

I remember once sitting with Ric in the afternoon, discussing the failure of his tenants to pay their rents promptly.

Fucking jokers, he called them.

Not you squire, he said. You pay on time. You got respect. But the others…

He voice trailing off into a wheezy whisper.

Some a these clowns, he mumbled, you wouldn't

believe.

He occasionally took me with him when he collected rents. Told me that my presence added a touch of class.

They look at me, he said, and see what they see. A lowlife. A rent collector. But you, you got a way about you. You bring a little distinction to the party.

Ric was a man constantly on the hustle. His money blew in and slipped out, he gambled, he speculated, he ventured; he was a chancer. He once held up a twenty pound note and said, whatta going to do with it? Eat it? Wear it? Fill it with petrol and drive it around? Hang it on your wall?

He folded it into his pocket and said, best thing to do with it is let it circulate.

Money, he said, is pure animal business. It can't stand to be caged. Can't abide pockets or banks or wallets. You gotta release it into the wild. Let it be what it is. Let it do what it's going to do. Who wants a buncha tame ass money laying around the place? Better to let it be feral, better to let it have teeth and claws and let it draw blood. Let it roam and be disorderly. That's what money is.

We once went to collect some rent from a man named Segg. The man had offices in the West End above a photographer. From the photographer, said Ric, I get no pain. He pays. He tells me nothing and I ask nothing. He keeps his curtains drawn. God knows what goes on. He points and clicks and gives me what's mine. This fella Segg is another kettle of fish. This fella complains. Tells me his business is slow and so the rent will be thin but he'll add it on to next months. Which never comes. Every month there's a story. A new baby or a sick wife or a leaky roof or a dying aunt. Every month there's a disaster. Every month he sends me a few pennies and the latest installment of My Sorry Life.

We climbed the stairs and arrived at a door that had Mr. Hayward Segg, Imports And Exports written on it. We didn't knock. We stepped in and found Segg behind a disheveled desk. Segg was shorter than he thought he was. He did his best to look like someone in the movies, Oliver Reed maybe, or an angered Alan Bates. He leant back and squinted at Ric, as if looking through a narrow window.

Ric, he said, to what do I owe the pleasure?

Ric didn't say anything, just took a note book and tape measure from his pocket and started measuring the room. He measured one wall and wrote something on his pad.

Segg rose and asked, whattaya doing?

Ric said nothing, just continued around the room, measuring and making notes.

Segg took a step around the desk and said, what's all this?

Still Ric was silent. He measured the doors and windows, he flipped the lights on and off, he shook his head as if making complicated calculations.

When Segg approached him Ric finally turned and, as if seeing Segg for the first time, said, whatta you still doing here?

Whattaya mean? This is my office.

Is it? Far as I know an office is something you pay rent for and as I haven't had any rent in four months I assumed you'd left and that was that. I thought you were long gone. Far as I know I'm free to let this office to someone new.

He nodded in my direction.

I've brought someone round who needs an office and I've made promises and I didn't expect to find you here and you've put me in difficult position.

He looked at me again and asked, whattaya reckon? This enough space for you?

I nodded.

Good. I'm assuming it'll be cleared by the end of the week. That right Segg?

Segg, as if caught in a stiff wind, stepped backward and held up his hands.

You can't do this Ric. You can't push me out.

I can do, Ric said, whatever I like with my own property. Especially that property that's currently unpaid for.

Segg's bluster was spent. He looked like what he was, a small time hustler in need of a drink. He sat in his chair and looked at Ric's feet. His shoulders sagged.

I never thought you'd be like this Ric.

Ric smiled and said, like what?

Segg leaned over his desk, opened a deep drawer and removed a metal box. He opened it and began counting out notes.

Like blood from a stone, he said. Like blood from a bloody stone.

He handed Ric a stack of bills, closed the box and grumbled, you're killing me Ric.

Ric turned to me and said, I'm afraid there's been an unforeseen turn of events and the office is no longer available. Please accept my apologies.

I did my best to look disappointed.

Bev falls asleep immediately, in a muttering heap. She leans into me, pushes against my left arm and is gone. Whilst I remain awake and on the prowl. My blood may be weak but my mind is willing. It barges about the place, dredging. Spinning, rambling, blathering; while the boat gentles against the bank. I wish there was a window. There must be, somewhere, stars. A moon too and planets. The Milky Way. At the very least bats and night hawks. Instead I count ceiling planks. Forty three. I squeeze in closer to Bev.

He was not my friend. He was, very much, my father. He inhabited a different world. A world of which I was aware, I knew its precincts and basic rules, I knew some of its geography, but its local customs, its loyalties, were beyond me. He lived in the adult world alone; he had colleagues, he had peers, he had, occasionally, clients, but the bulk of his time was spent alone. In the evenings and for a short moment each morning, we crossed into a shared borderland. He addressed me with deference, with respect; his gentleness was absolute. He assumed and expected the same gentleness in others. He was mostly disappointed.

The books I read then, the science fiction of the fifties, were an unlikely world into which I snuck. I bought them cheaply and treated them accordingly. They were a far shore onto which my father would never stray. They were as far away as it was possible to be from his arrangements of cups and jars.

Bev purrs and turns onto her side. I'm not, and have never been, equal to her. As nothing is equal to any other thing. There was a time, when we were first knowing each other, that it was most acute. That I struggled to be brighter. Brushing my hair and memorising quotes. Wearing socks that matched my jumper. Saying things I hoped, one day, to believe. Cultivating a general sense of worthiness. I wanted to impress her; instead I was permanently riled and unwashed. I was nowhere near her and it played on me. I wanted to say, sure I'm unkempt and my thoughts aren't much but most days I do one good thing. I wanted to say: I'm trying. I wanted to say: I'm trying *for you*. Now, thirty years later, still unequal, still a failer, it all feels less weighty. My concerns have become other. I began, at some point, to worry less. About less. Perhaps I reached the limits of my understanding. Perhaps my ulcer reordered my priorities. Perhaps I bumped against something unseen; I seem now to be concerned with old things in new ways. My feet, my nose, the glands that pack my underarms, my relationship to automobiles and porridge, the way I enter a room hazily, without intent. My suspicions concerning most dogs and all horses. My afflicted need for Bev. It's all familiar but familiar in new ways. I find myself wondering what it is to be her body. Her arms and eyebrows. Her hips and guts. The household of her insides. How are they organised? Are they all of an allegiance? She seems more of a whole than I. The various sides of her acting in accordance. She once asked me, Mouse, why do you look at me that way? and I, speechless, couldn't tell her that she blinded me.

There was a book I once read, when I was growing, that imagined a world where people were allowed to live fifty years from any given moment. Only fifty. They had to pin point a moment and say this is it, this is my moment, and they were given fifty more years, but at exactly that same age. They neither aged nor changed. No additional weight, no creakings. They were as they were for fifty years and then they were dead. Ultimately, because most people, being humdrum and predictable, chose a moment in their early twenties, when they thought they looked and smelled their best, the civilisation collapsed. How could a world of youth, born of certainty and speed, survive?

I put my arm over her hip. Warm she is and egg smooth. My taxes, let's be honest, are a mess. I've lived all my adult life in fear of exposure. Lying not for gain but from boredom. I make up figures that sound, and look, reasonable. I start with the best of intentions, I spread out the forms and position my envelopes of receipts, I add up my profits and subtract my expenses and I get through a couple months; then I get bored. My eyes shutter and my blood, my weak blood, turns sluggish. I can't be bothered. I throw together a few likely numbers and hope.

Another book of my youth imagined a scientist who had solved the problem of time travel, albeit only backwards and only for a few hours. It soon became evident that, contrary to what his fellow scientists (and writers and theorists) thought, history was a solid, linear, fossilised thing. Once a thing had happened it could not unhappen. People could go back in time and act with impunity; nothing they did there would in any way effect the world they had left. The scientist, as the scientists in those books always did, sold his invention to a company that promised to use it for the good of mankind.

They didn't. The past, very quickly, became a play-ground, a holiday destination. People went back and forth, living a second chance. They were able to love, commit murder, seduce, placate, connive, enslave, create; and then return to a present where nothing had changed. The relationship between action and reaction was severed. The scientist was appalled and eventually became a haunted wreck, constantly revisiting the past, destroying his lab and all his experiments, then returning to a present full of people with no sense of accountability.

I was schooled by my father's disappointments. He taught me how to roll my shoulders in a way that said, I have nothing further to add. He taught me absence, he taught me those things that are assumed unteachable. He taught in an over voweled, mooing way. Looking at an unfinished canvas he'd tilt back and say, aaaaahh, oooooh, aaaye. His cuff linked sleeves tired and oil stained. His wire framed glasses milky. He'd ask me, pointing at a salt cellar or a biscuit tin, what do you think I've done wrong? His eyes, behind his milky glasses, sharp as finches.

We went, on Sunday afternoons, to a local park. There was a grandstand there, and grass, and chairs, and a booth where they sold tea and doughnuts. There were dogs too and children on bicycles; also, near the river, a plaque in honour of a heroic schoolboy. The schoolboy having saved his two brothers and a dog from a burning barge.

His name was Watkins and this was in the time of
Dickens. A time, my father said, when sizes were
different. Big wasn't nearly so big and small was
much smaller. Tall meant something not so terribly tall and short meant tiny. My father also said:
Dickens used an awful lot of words to say a simple
thing. Having just read A Tale Of Two Cities in
school I was inclined to agree.

We entered the park at its south east corner.
The same place every Sunday. Quietly near the
herbaceous borders. We were the kind who stepped
lightly, making eye contact with no one. Here we
are, my father would whisper and I, pleased to be
out in the world with him, by his side, would agree:
yes, here we are.

There amongst the Sundayers, the town folk.
The voters who thought: the park and all herein
is ours. They strolled, they loitered, they lounged
near the duck pond. They were in possession of
their free time. We were nothing to them. We were
left to roam in a ghostly fashion, floating several
inches above the graveled paths. First north to the
sheep fields, then west along the river, then south
around the football pitch, and finally east, back to
our entry gate. During this final leg we stood for
some minutes looking out at the river; at the ducks,
the swans, the squirrels, the drifting bits of wood.
Never once did we use the public toilets. We each
wore glasses and tweed caps and knit scarves. My
hair, around the ears, longer. My boots, around

the soles, more worn. Occasionally, if the day was sufficiently cold or sufficiently damp, we bought, from the man near the grandstand, four doughnuts in a brown paper bag.

Bev in the moonlight grumbles. Her knee angles into my back. She turns and whispers. She is, inside, a whole person. Wet and complete. A person I sometimes know. Who periodically changes shape in order to accommodate new things. Her spleen and kidneys shift, her stomach shrinks, her liver makes room for disappointment and intrigue, her bladder for some new taste. While I am what I have always been, hardened; King Tut, in my sandstone lair. Each day, in London, after her morning cello practice, she swam. Sixty lengths in the Camberwell Baths. In a black second skin with goggles and cap. She was and is trim. As are greyhounds, as are fish and garden snakes.

My greatest fear then, in those early days, was that she might die or disappear or somehow be made permanently vacant, leaving me alone and vulnerable. It was a thought that caused me much stomach upset and localized hair loss. A small minded selfishness of which I wasn't ashamed. I wanted her at my side and why not? Was I not entitled to desire?

And now, forty years later, here we are, floating in a strange bed, still together and look: still alone, still fearful, still vulnerable.

I'm mostly a shallow man. I toy with big ideas but mostly I'm lazy. I steal strength from those I love, those I remember, that which I admire. A succubus. With little or no self generated contribution.

Another childhood book: a spectacular cover, silver writing on a purple planet, set against an orange sky. The story of an interplanetary policeman and his affair with a shape shifter, a being whose appearance changed depending on ancient and unpredictable cycles. First it was one thing and then another, people of both sexes and varying ages, plants both native and foreign, talking dogs, a variety of skittish highland beasts. Finally, having come home to a chimpanzee waiting in the front room, the policeman asked, who, exactly, are you?

I am what I am, was the answer.

Eventually, at the behest of the exhausted and bewildered policeman, they parted.

His life resumed its former dullness. He did what policemen do. He lived with order and constraint. Gone was his one point of excitement, of unknowableness. He regretted ending the affair. The story ended with him wandering the galaxy, lonely and disconsolate, accosting strangers and their pets with the repeated phrase: are you her? Are you? Are you her?

There was another book that imagined a planet where a lifespan was measured in language. Each being was allotted, on birth, a set number of words. When these words were all used, all spoken, the person died. Words were gold. Or beyond gold. The building blocks of being. Suicide was accomplished in a storm of speech. Old age was the exclusive domain of the reticent. There were rumours of an ancient people, in a far sanctuary, beyond time and age, who had never spoken.

I guess that what I'm saying is this: these books left their mark.

Come the morning I haven't slept. What I've done is create an alphabet of shapes beneath the blanket. Denied sleep I was and able only to play my games. Count backwards from one hundred, imagine blank walls, white depeopled places, slow my breath to a shallow wheeze. Pretend. Nothing helped. Nothing does. Who among us, at three o-clock in the morning, has ever been helped? Name one. Name one beneficiary. One for whom helped ever arrived. The night being, in most cases, a brute. Crowded and base smelling. A holeish place.

Bev, oblivious, who *has* slept, who *is* revived, who smells irritatingly of lavender, looks at me with distaste and says, you look awful.

To which I snort. A snort that means: of course I look awful. I am awful. I'm old and sluggish and have an ulcer that refuses to heal. And my hip here, where I've lain eight hours on my side, unsleeping, hurts.

Something hard bodied and thin winged is repeatedly hurling itself against the glass. A bee? A wasp? A large fly? No weak blood there. The window being one of two half circles; admitting smudgy light. It, whatever it is, keeps sizzling around the place. The problem, I accept, concerning last nights performance, is my refusal to accept the night as disorderly. There's a need in me to neaten, to make tidy. To arrange. As with my father and his cups, his jugs, his Wedgewood plates. Perhaps as a defense against the untidiness of dreams. I would prefer, if it were an option, to sit quietly for eight hours. Eyes open, hands clasped, neither listening nor watching. Bev is in the kitchen, assembling her muesli, her toast, her tea. Nothing for poor old weak blooded, awful looking me. She's humming something imperfect and lazy. I'm left here in bed, amongst the bugs. I struggle up and remove my pajamas, stand for a moment and of course Bev is right. I look awful. As do most men in my condition. I sag. Old, weakened, invaded. A collection of teeth, knees, knuckles, belly. No strength left in me, no urgency. I dress in the same clothes I've worn for fifty years; I do not, cannot, look in the mirror. I pivot the window wider and wait. When the bug comes coptering, I make whooshing motions that don't help. I've opened the fucking window, I tell it, pointing. I follow it around the room muttering.

Finally it alights on the glass and I push it into the day. A wasp of the thin, long legged variety. That may or may not have stung me if given the chance. The day is plump and bulgy, showy. Clouds and all that. I climb the three steps out of the bedroom one at a time, slowly, already short-breathed.

4

You know why I quit playing ballads?
Cause I love playing ballads.

So said Miles Davis.

I hear voices that are not immediately involved in my napping dreams. From the bow of the boat. The dream concerning, in some way, a crowded room in which several people are wearing hats made from skinned rabbits. Of the kind often pictured on Vikings. With heads and tails intact. The hats being all there is in terms of clothing – the crowd being mostly naked. The dream mingles with the birdsong and whatnot. The voices are discussing miles and maps and destinations; where we are and where we're going. One voice, unknown to me, is saying, maybe fifteen miles. Give or take. No more than twenty. And Bev is saying: I guess that's it then. Settled. That's where we're going.

So something, in my absence, is being decided. Action is being taken. A plan, as they say, is being hatched. All without consulting Mr. Mediocre Ulcer Man. So no change there.

This daytime napping, these small collapses, ten minutes here, twenty minutes later, mid-morning, after lunch, is what I do now. How I go about things. I've become a snoozer, a forty winkser. My blood gets overwhelmed and there I go; I poop out. I cease, for a few minutes, to be. Mouth open, teeth and gums exposed, a light dribble on my shirt. Except, of course, at night. At night I piss and moan and am very much not a snoozer. At night I become a rememberer.

Old age being a thing with which I have little in common. By which I mean: I am one thing, old age is something else. Something very much not me. By which I mean: we are not, though it would seem otherwise, conjoined. Old age has its agenda, I have mine. I have a lifetime of shit inside. I've seen stuff, watched it, had it do things to me, unspeakable things. I've been *me*. Old age is a late comer, a gatecrasher, someone uninvited whom I've never met but who now won't leave.

I make my way to the bow where two things are thrown at me. One, Bev is wearing a hat I've never seen and two, we have a visitor. I'm more intrigued by the hat than the visitor. A broad brimmed affair with a tie under her chin. In swirling purples and yellows. Orange too and turquoise stripes. With a paper flower on one side. Who in their right mind would wear such a thing? Where did it come from? I stand speechless, requiring an explanation: how has such an abomination come to rest on her head?

I point a shaking finger at it and she smiles. Found it under the bed, she says.

Which makes it even worse. Not only is it hideous, it's trash.

I like it, she says. Summery.

Is it? I ask and she turns away, giving it a gentle pat.

Our visitor, assuming a Roman pose, leans against the boat. One hand resting on a walking stick, the other spread across his chest. An unimportant belly, sloppy shoulders. Plum coat. Many zippered knapsack. Sunglasses staring straight up at the sun, atop his head. Black, of the kind that hide everything. And boots of a military origin. An umbrella too, strapped to his walking stick. He points down the canal at nothing. A horse, unseen behind the hedge, neighs.

I had once, briefly, a school friend. The friend who loaned me the Miles Davis record. We were fifteen and I thought I knew something about him. I watched him scuttle between classes, noted the titles of his books, listened to him discuss the shortcomings of various public minded charities. His father was a gardener, his mother was interested in multi-purpose compost and little else. We were acquainted for just over two years. We were never close. I watched him keep himself separate from other people; I thought that good practice. As we had little in common, we began, in a small way, shoplifting. It seemed a reasonable pursuit. We'd sit in his room listening to records, dividing what we'd stolen; sweets, magazines, boxes of matches, rubber balls; nothing we wanted. He planned to be a journalist. He mentioned the UN and peace keeping missions and the need for a united Europe. He carried with him, at all times, a book by George Orwell. There was about him a peculiar smell, impervious to soap; the stink of damp wool.

He began, slowly, to complicate his desires; he got an apprenticeship with a local paper; he acquired a pipe. I saw nothing of him for ten years.

When I was in my late twenties, married, settling into McPherson's, possessed of unclear yearnings, I sought him out. He too had moved to London and was living in Soho, over a house of prostitutes, on a street flooded with grubby water; I stood for awhile watching the flickering windows, ignoring the noises that leaked from within. The names listed on the buzzers were Crystal, Victoria, Melody, Bethany and there, at the top, Rogers. A hand written note said: Due to ill health Joanna is no longer seeing clients. There were no street lights.

I had thought, when I made enquiries as to his whereabouts, that his influence might force me to become more explicitly myself. I might look to him for clues. I was in the process of initiating a thorough review of whom I wanted to be. I hoped he might bring me into the world. I occasionally saw his byline in a national paper. I pointed them out to Bev. She called him Mr. Front Page. I never, in the end, summoned the courage to talk to him. His

Soho flat, his slight renown, the often angry tone of his writing, it was all too brutal, too severe. I never approached him. I lacked the necessary pluck. I noticed that his articles lessened and five years later he was dead, of a heroin overdose; I went to a memorial service where a colleague told me: he spoiled the one good thing he had. I sat amongst people I'd never met mourning a man I'd never really known.

Well, well, my father said, upon meeting Bev.

This wasn't long after her, and my, youth had ebbed away. Or those clothes, those mornings, those fizzy drinks, that I counted as youth. Those bright pajamas and ferment. An attachment to certain books and movies. The establishment of body hair and bulk around the middle. Such was, at the time, my way of thinking. Believing as I did in firmly established thresholds. We were, it seemed, entering a new world. Goodbye youth, hello insight. The gates opened, the mechanisms sprung. We were, it turned out, entering nothing of the sort. We were entering more of the same. We were as we had always been. As we would always be. As we still are. We had told my father that we might like to get married. Tie the knot, was the phrase Bev used. The words, to us, immense. Once said, impossible to unsay. My father had quietly coughed and said (again), well, well. Bev, I think, would have liked more. We outlined, in broad strokes, our plans.

We had no plans. We had nearly nothing. We had each other. We had a mutual distrust of children. We each, in different ways, enjoyed silence. We were fond of paella. Neither of us were particularly excitable. Music, in different ways, featured. As I said, nearly nothing. We each stared intently at the ground. Then my father pushed at a loose lock of hair and said, it's important in life not to out stay ones welcome.

She had neither parents nor memory of parents. Only a foster mother who had died when Bev was eighteen. That's it, she told me. That's the whole entire story. No one then and no one now. Until you.

That night, in our underlit, unordered kitchen, she told me, I think I like your father a little bit more than I like you.

She smiled and said, and I like you a great deal.

I wasn't displeased.

We had, as a celebration, a box of Russian pastries. Of the kind filled with dates and roasted almonds.

Your father, Bev said, lifting a wedge to her mouth, is not one to be toyed with.

I must have looked confused because she gave my forehead a tap-tap and whispered: don't give me that squirrelly look mister, you know exactly what I mean.

Our visitor stands on the path, looking down

the canal. He makes it clear that his world is the world of the walker. We float, he walks. His boots are well used. His legs sturdy. He has about him the look of miles. He says something about setting off, about being on his way.

Bev nods and says, you need a cup of tea?

What I'm thinking is: let's start again. Reset. Can we do that? I'll walk back to the bedroom, lie down, have a little nap, dream about Viking headwear, wake up, walk back to the bow and find Bev alone, reading, dehatted, unbefriended, among the water bugs and dragon flies.

Instead I stand. I count to twenty and then retreat to the rudder. Bev puts one hand on top of her new hat and the Roman says, thanks but no. He gives us a regal wave and strides off down the path. Bev flips a switch and things happen. We tilt, slightly, wheezing towards the centre of the canal. I give a weak blooded salute and off we go, west, I suppose towards Wales, towards the sea, towards this afternoon, away from last night, into that which will be.

There was a time when I assumed McPherson's was forgotten. As are minor players in popular films. As are the dates of certain civil war battles. As are certain mid-century painters. Unremembered. Disappeared. Passed over. It was an assumption that suited me. I went years without a visit from Ric. My bank paid his bank. I received neither receipt nor response. I assumed that Ric was either in jail or abroad. I had no concrete evidence for this, just neighbourhood whispers. I asked for nothing from Ric and received it. In my dank burrow without even a sink, without a toilet. With the wood lice and black, hairy legged centipedes. Without either a kettle or computer. King of a sodden country. When a letter came demanding a much raised rent, from (the letter said) the new owners of the building, what could I do? What could I say? Am I a fighter? A negotiator? Do I possess even a hint of moxie? Have I ever, at any time, raised either my voice or my fists? Me, the overlooked. I didn't even reply. I emitted a quiet grunt and closed early. Put a SALE sign in the window and let my regulars take what they could carry. Forty years wrapped up in two days. Mcpherson's chair, the record player, the posters of Archie Shepp and Sun Ra, the framed pictures of Theodore Sturgeon and Philip K. Dick, all left behind. I turned out the weak lights and propped up a farewell letter on the counter: To Whom It May Concern – As you will discover, there are things living down here, ghosts and what have you, wood worm and mice, that mostly, given good intentions and gentleness, won't hurt you. Mostly they keep to themselves. The ghosts are of a benevolent nature; they watch but don't join in. For thirty years we've sold books here and ghosts come with the territory. Be good to these three rooms, they're small and airless and feel slightly like those boxes people move cats in, but they're decent rooms, they mean no harm, they have, mostly, kept out the worst of what the world offers. We did what we did here quietly and hurt no one. Best of luck and welcome.

This ulcer business came at me after I quit the shop. Perhaps in response to myself being removed even further from the world. Why, my body seemed to say, do you need a healthy innards if you plan to retreat? Withdrawal has no need for vigor. If you plan to whither, my body said, do it with a leaky stomach. This was before the internet infected the guts of the world. I must remember to be thankful that I spent the majority of my life before that happened. I was simply a bookseller and the shop was only a shop. What we did there was done only there. It wasn't, as book shops are now, a front for something else entirely. We had, and sought, no other options. At McPherson's everything we had was on the shelves. In thirty years I posted nothing. I served no coffee. I baked no muffins. If you wanted obscure French texts on post structuralism, or books with lurid covers concerning life on distant planets, McPherson's was your place.

And if you wanted me, the bookseller, the silent one, the mouse, the jazz lover, the rememberer, you came around to see me. You sought me out. Your pushed open the door, descended the stairs and waited while I turned down the music. You conducted your business within arm's length. We faced each other. We said what needed to be said. We didn't haggle. You gave me money. I thanked you. I bagged your book and off you went.

It was in the empty weeks after we closed that I visited my doctor, complaining of stomach pains. My doctor friend rested his fingers against my loosened and speckled neck. Just enough pressure to feel my liquid insides. He was so minty. In his too clean office. I dared not breathe too deeply. His fingers were just below my left ear.

Something funny here. He said. Looking at his watch. In his white coat and strawberry bow tie.

Weary? he asked. In your bones?

Weary, I said, unto death.

I also said something about my sleeplessness, my nerves, my sudden and violent dislike of apples.

Your pulse, he said, isn't exactly what you might call hammering.

I nodded and he removed his fingers.

When have I ever been, I asked, a crash, boom, bang kinda guy?

His smile turned into something unsmiley. He tapped the corner of his desk and gave me a slow nod. He was, I knew, troubled. I, or my blood, was troubling him. I had brought, into this clean and bright room, trouble.

Bev takes over the rudder and I slump at her side. She strokes the top of my head. If I could purr I would. Or perhaps wag a tail. I grunt.

Do we, I ask, know where we're going?

We're going a little bit west, she says. And mostly south.

I try to nod but it's too much effort. I'm at the mercy of the air, Bev's hand, the sound of the water. I'm all drowsy. I do that thing old people do, I die a little bit.

I close my eyes and there's my father. In our house in the hills. The house of his father. And mother. Also, at times, his aunt Bella. All of whom died when I was an infant.

My father never got old. Never did he falter. No arthritis or forgetfulness. No drooling. He seemed to be always the same; a middling kind of middle age. He was able and skilled and overly precise in his manners. And then he wasn't.

His father, mother and aunt all died within weeks of each other, of whatever flu was popular that year. This was in the olden days and things like that happened then. An exotic strain of flu knocked on the door and wiped out the entire household. Who had easy access to buckets of penicillin? A few sniffles, a sneeze, a cough, a fever, and that's it, time's up. It was neither a bad stomach nor the flu that did for my father. It was a truck full of timber. It was speed and metal and a loose hat. He was on his morning walk beside a country road when, according to the driver, he lost his hat to a gust of wind. He turned to catch it, tripped, and fell into the street. And that was very much that. An instant goner.

When I visited the spot the next day there was a fist sized stain on the road. Blood of my father. When I visited again, a week later, it was gone. Grubbed into the road with the other oil stains and dank puddles.

We nudge into and through a stand of birches. It feels as if we've been swallowed, as if we're inside the insides of something, the trees being the bone white ribs. The trees, these specific tress, that grow along this canal, are slowly dying. I read about them last week. A woman wearing a t-shirt that said Love Our Waterways was handing out leaflets. A small woman with large eyes. I liked the look and idea of her but could work up no enthusiasm to talk to her. I learned, reading her leaflet, that microscopic beads of carcinogenic plastic are entering the root systems and slowly rotting the trees from the inside out. Rather like my torn stomach. The carcinogens being the result of pesticides and silage from over farmed fields. The carcinogens being what we leave behind. Our foot print. Our way of saying thank you to those things that are both most vulnerable and most needed.

We are not good neighbours.

Or, perhaps, some of us are not good neighbours. I've had a father, a wife, customers, a doctor; I've given people money, taken money from them;

I've conversed, sometimes at length, about the weather, about politics, about the paucity of local services. I've both received and been given help. I realize I'm not alone. I live amongst my own kind. Chin to chin and toe to toe. I nod, I smile, I ignore them; sometimes, for unthinking reasons, I say good morning.

Never have I had mates. Never sat in a pub. Never discussed the football. My sexual exploits have never been detailed. Never have I been slapped fondly on the back. Never been fishing or hiking or played golf. Never have I done whatever it is that mates do.

I have, at times, been trapped in situations that demand a certain level of interaction with strangers. These strangers are in and of the world in a way that is unimaginable to me. They have their families, cars, jobs, mortgages, pensions, hobbies, affairs, passions; they have a certain weight. They have ready gadgets. They talk without fear.

I have never been certain of my place in that world. The world does not move with me nor me with it. I am at the foot of something steep.

A successful day is one that doesn't end in public humiliation.

Bev keeps us on course. The course offering little in the way of options. Bev keeps us away from the sides and pointed west. She hums. A canal being, for each narrow boat, a one way deal. You go in the direction you're pointed. You can't turn around. The boat's too long, the canal's too narrow. You proceed until you stop proceeding. It's a boat fit for only one purpose. Being neither sleek nor nimble; covering between fifteen and twenty miles a day. Or less, depending on the number of locks you encounter. Traveling at roughly three miles an hour. The rule is: if you're making waves you're going too fast.

5

Whatever happens will be for the worse,
and therefore it is in our interest that
as little should happen as possible.

So said Lord Salisbury.

I t's salad tonight. Bev's turn and Bev doesn't
cook; she assembles. Slivers of green and red
and something darker, leafier, together with broad
beans and sweet corn. Olive oil and lemon juice.
On another plate rice cakes. Of the kind flavoured
with pepper and sea salt. And we've got hummus
and chutney. She has wine and I have water. Soon
she'll start her celloing.

I can feel my weak blood sludging around my
body. Up and across my shoulders, around my
wearied head, the length of my arms, down and
back up my legs, the complicated swirl of my guts.
It creeps. I don't begrudge it its fatigue. Who am I
to judge, to expect better? It's been doing the same
old pump and pulse for a long time. Never a rest,
never a break. Up and down the same old body,
the same relentless route, in and out of the same
passages. And if finally, after all these years, it's less
than enthusiastic in its chores, who am I to argue?
If it cheats and misses out the extremities, the toes

and fingers, the nose, who am I to demand more? I let it be what it is. I collect the plates and swish them in the canal.

To the left sweeps a tuft of willow branches. The leaves thin and yellow and then not so thin but still yellow, the water black. There are ducks out there, multi coloured, gliding around in circles. The air, in the country style, is manured.

I look down and watch a couple of corn kernels and a streak of salad dressing go swirly. A treat for the fish. I walk slowly to the kitchen and open the tiny window. It's then that I hear him. An indistinct hum from the bow. Bev laughing. I put away the plates and sit down. More than ever my single wish is to be left alone. Just me and Bev and my ulcer. My shoulders that ache, my fingers that throb, my knees that click. I want a world no bigger than this boat. Populated by only Bev, myself and my rememberings. I'm an old, slow, man. I stand and wobble towards the bow. Past the willows and the ducks. I round the cabin and there he is. The walker with the belly. The Roman. Leaning on his stick sharing a joke with Bev.

I realize that what I want may not be what Bev wants. I'm sure it's not. What two people ever wanted the exact same thing? She wants what she wants, I want what I want. I want less. I want solitude. I want long unlanguaged stretches. She, perhaps, wants company. Perhaps raised glasses and gossip. Perhaps shoes that involve heels and thin straps.

As I said, I assume nothing. She's a surpriser.

Mr. Belly is facing east, his face shadowed. He sees me and waves. Says, howdy.

Bev tilts her head and says, Mouse, come meet Poole.

I step over to the rail and Mr. Belly extends his hand; I'm left with no alternative. I shake it.

Poole Blount. He says.

I whisper my name and various things are said, some by Poole, some by Bev. Tea is offered and accepted, biscuits are mentioned, the weather is praised, an invitation to come on board is issued. I stand back and watch things happen.

Bev, when Bev was younger, used to say, there's no way I should be sitting here. Meaning with me, the kind of person I was, in our flat, saying the kinds of things we said, wearing what we wore, eating what we ate. In matching chairs that were there when we moved in. On either side of a radiogram. On the rose carpet that had pulled away at the corners. In the empty evenings that were shaped by Radio 3. Meaning that she had never considered a life like the one she had.

Who ever imagines the life they eventually have?

A favourite pastime being this: imagining histories for the parents she never knew. It gave her, momentarily, the narrative she lacked. It was a game we played there in our dim flat. Her parents (she might say), had money that they spent on things that meant little to them. Fashionable shoes and exotic house plants and cocktails. They were proliferate. They had opinions that ran contrary to good taste. They were of the kind that spent and bought and lived until, in a heap, they had nothing. They were then a nuisance to their friends. In a moment of carelessness she became pregnant. Almost certainly by him. They lived for a short time in reduced circumstances. The baby was dealt with, put up for adoption and gone. They each tried, with no success, to earn a living. Writing, banking, acting, selling. Nothing worked. Both died suddenly and thankfully, in the house of a distant cousin, he of liver failure, she of cancer.

Perhaps they were (she might say) barely familiar. Drink and optimism had been involved. The music too, of a popular dance band. She a singer, he a trumpet player. They rendezvoused in the back room of a church hall. It had been rash and reckless, an experiment, but it was done and could not then be undone. It was, in the way of those times, involving priests and well meaning widows, dealt with.

Or perhaps they were not as they should have been (she might say). He married, she not. He willing, she not. He careless, she not. A mismatch. A kilter that was very much off. It was said that he had money and was overly close to his mother. It was also said, about her, that she was inexperienced and without imagination. That she was a beauty but took no pleasure in it. He was twenty years her elder. A civil servant. A man with ways and means. A man who, through official channels and monied luncheons, dealt with it.

She is and was a bird shaped woman. A song maker. One of the garden types, of the slight, green variety. Tiny feet, a solid but hollow boned body, a small head. Heard more often than seen. She perches. Music patiently gathers around her; it matters in an unlettered way. It matters forever. She is and was on the side of those who carried the least weight.

You hear that? she'd ask, listening to something medieval, pointing at the radio. Did you hear that?

I would shake my head and she, in the gloom, would say, the way the bass viol drew across the E string and held the minor chord.

Full of admiration she was. Aaaahhh, she'd whisper.

She knew that my enjoyment came from watching her enjoyment. The subtleties lost on me. We often lit candles and lay on the floor, the music floating up there with the cobwebs and dust, near the ceiling. Bev would sometimes hum along and I liked that. Sometimes I rubbed her feet and she liked that. We weren't of the kind that demanded much.

We argued once over a painting of my father's. The painting, of a soup tureen, a tea cup and an empty vase, was called Arrangement 137. It was featured in an exhibition at the Whitechapel Gallery. The catalogue for the exhibition, entitled English Modernists And Other Malcontents, included short biographies of each artist. My father's read: Herbert Hillier (1907 – 1961) lived and worked in mid-Wales. A master of light and shade, Hillier was often called "a Welsh Morandi." While his early work reflected his friendships with members of the Vorticists, his later work was more singular, based on the constant examination and reworking of domestic household implements. There are examples of his paintings in several important collections. He lived alone, with neither partner nor children.

Bev was horrified. She perched and fluttered.

Neither partner nor children?

I shrugged it off. A mistake. Who cares?

I care, she said.

Family, I knew, meant something very different to her than it did to me. We were different people. We felt different things. People, even those as close as Bev and I, or perhaps especially those as close as Bev and I, live differently. (Can I admit to being a little bit thrilled at that sentence: He lived alone, with neither partner nor children? I felt the freedom of sovereignty. I was, with a single sentence, unshackled from my past. I was in no way proud of feeling that way.) I told Bev, what does it matter? I know he was my father. I know how I felt about him. I know what kind of life we had.

Bev pouted.

It's not fair. She said. To him, to you, to us.

At which point, as if I knew nothing of Bev and her weaknesses, let alone my own weaknesses, as if we'd never met, I did the exact wrong thing. I laughed.

Bev, her eyes filmed, thwarted, touched my arm and said, really?

When it's later Poole, who's been drinking wine from a collapsible cup, is talking about celestial pathways. Bev is nodding her little bird head. Around us the night huddles. We've had him all day. Or Bev has had him. I've had a nap and read a book and been pointedly disinterested. There's no moon to speak of, the stars too are few. Up there it's mostly just a big black hole. Down here there's us, the boat, the canal, the willow. No farm house lights, no passing cars. There's a breeze, barely moving, nudging the boat. On the table are three hissing candles. Bev and Poole are sitting in the folding chairs while I'm over here by the rail, on the bench, drowsing. I notice a blinking light that's inching slowly left to right. I watch it stutter. An airplane I suppose. Or satellite. Metal and glass and wired bits that have no business in heaven.

The patterns of space travel, says Poole, exist outside the terms of our reasoning. Space travel is outside man, outside humanity, and therefore outside human pettiness, human slyness, human spite and viciousness, outside the battle cry of give me, give me, give me.

His voice is of the kind people call sonorous. Is that the word? Meaning low and full and of a commanding nature? His cadence is unrushed, he lays down words as if distributing dominoes. I lose, at times, the precise meaning of it. The overall impression is of a serious nature.

Man, he says, has made little effort to be better.

We all agree. Bev and I nod, the wind nods, the willow and the water nod, the night, as if all of one being, nods.

It's space travel for a minute and then celestial pathways and then it's something else. I kind of keep up. Bev nods and pecks at her wine. Then it's God.

God, he says, the great space traveler Yahweh, told us 'Thou shalt not kill' and we, ungrateful delinquents, killed him.

He says this simply, without affect.

All night, at irregular intervals, I hear him, from where he's curled beneath the table, snoring like a wounded woodland animal. It's not an unpleasant sound. It's the sound of a living thing, recharging. I imagine him gathering berries from the hedgerow and eating them delicately, one at a time. I'm thinking gooseberries or blackberries, something that involves thorns. I see him lumbering, scaring hikers, going on his way in an unhurried fashion. He feels like someone dislodged from normal life.

Someone who, at some specific point, fell into a way of being in direct opposition to everything that had gone before. An engineer perhaps, or a mechanic, a university lecturer; someone who had turned his ample back on whatever life he had.

These things happen. I know that. They also don't happen. I know that a single word or gesture, an unknown whim, a seemingly casual desire can be the catalyst for total change.

When Bev, in the seventh year of our marriage, met Dave, a fellow cellist, it was touch and go for a while. She flitted first here and then there. It was unclear with whom she wished to be. Time both stopped and sped. We both talked and were silent. Dave lived somewhere north of Camden, with a wife. It was complicated. I know these things happen, you read about them and hear about them, in operas and in the papers, but when it did, when the time came, I did not do myself proud. I said awful things and cried. I whimpered. I was my mousey, noncommunicative self. Eventually, as if at some predetermined point, Dave vanished and that was that. Nothing more was discussed. We, and us, resumed.

I could never convert my father to any other jazz musician than Miles Davis. I tried and I failed. He listened intently to Coltrane, to Mingus, to Shepp; he shook his head and said, well, well. And that was that. Never again were they mentioned. He went back to his studio and his piles of well worn piano music; Bach, Chopin, Satie, Debussey, Faure. And occasionally, when required, Kind Of Blue.

My father fled from excess. He demanded less. Given a choice, he requested no choice. He saved himself for other things. His favourite story was of the violinist who sat at home playing the same note over and over for years. When asked why, he said: most people are searching for their note, I've found mine.

The only artist I remember him discussing with reverence was Hamada Tankei, a Japanese ceramicist who every week made the exact same bowl, the same height, the same circumference, the same glaze, the same weight. Fifty two a year for nearly ten years. There are, my father used to say, 486 Tankei bowls in the world and each one is different from every other one and yet each one is indistinguishable from the next. He said this with something approaching jealousy. His closet contained a selection of eight identical shirts, eight identical pairs of trousers, three identical suits, five identical cardigans, a stack of identical underwear, ten identical ties, twelve identical pairs of socks, three identical pairs of leather shoes. There are things, he seemed to be saying, that are worth thinking about, others that aren't. He knew, or thought he knew, what he wanted. He wanted space in which to be himself. He wanted a life cleared of unnecessary clutter. This included friends, art, music, language, clothes, and, in some unsaid, nuanced way, me. He wanted clear decks and empty calendars.

He wanted all of us in our places, and our places to smell soapy.

As usual, come morning, not having slept, I slept. While Bev did her tea/muesli/marmalade/toast thing. I heard her and I didn't hear her. Fetal as I was, curled around a pillow, venturing for a few fuzzy minutes into sleepland. When finally, over heated, I roused myself, I did so to the muted rumble of Poole talking, once again, about space travel.

The thing he's saying now is: there's nothing you can say about space travel that will, in any way, be right or correct. Because what you'll use is language and logic and science and ethics and all that human fiddle faddle that can't begin to understand the realms in which space travel occurs.

And I'm thinking: space travel already? So early in the morning?

Well, well, says Bev and Poole says, this stuff moves around outside the limits of our being.

I stand up and my blood, like thin, greasy soup, swashes around. I grab the corner of the door until it settles. My stomach is a constant niggling pain. Tiny bubbles pop behind my eyes. This is the way my body works now. After a moment I climb the steps and head for the voices. When I get to the bow Poole and Bev are engaged in some basic form of calisthenics. Each are bent at the waist, their arms stretched above their heads. They touch the ground (or in Poole's case a point twelve inches above the ground), straighten and repeat. All the time Poole is saying: it involves dimensions unknown to us. Seven, eight, nine dimensions. Not dimensions of form but dimensions of desire, dimensions of need. Dimensions that are brought into being by expectation.

Up they stand, down they bend. Up, down. Bev moves easily, as do stalks of grass, as do thin trees. As does smoke. It's lovely to watch the fold and crease of her.

Poole, less easily, says, now to the left.

They each straighten, raise their hands, tilt to the left, breath out, then return to the centre. Poole moves with a bulky gentleness. As, perhaps, a bear might. Or the Michelin man. Or certain Russian athletes.

And have you, asks Bev, (left) done any yourself (centre)? Of this space travelling (left)?

What *I've* done, says Poole, (centre) is a story best saved for another day.

He says this in a way that's both worrying and threatening. As if there are certain to be other days, other mornings, as if we now, the three of us, constitute a tribe; and as if there are things beyond telling, stories that can't be lipped, that are too tangled for talking, that are best unremembered. Stories about himself that are too damaging for mixed company.

Well, well. Says Bev.

An hour later we're three miles west and it's warmer, just a little, and all these outdoor things are happening; bugs and birds and little smeary cloudy stuff above. I'm on the rudder while Bev and Poole are feet up in the folding chairs, talking the way old friends talk, meanderingly, with long empty stretches.

I'm wondering if Bev has invited him along, if a formal invitation has been extended, if we now have a permanent quest, or if this, like the smeary clouds and bugs, is temporary.

We're all of us involved, he's saying, with myth making. Myth above, below, behind. Myth is the ground we walk on, the water that feeds it. Myth is the creator and the created. And the day will come when the myth takes over, when we'll shed our old ways and become the myth. You hear me? When we become ideas, pure energy, lightening bolts of chi, pure non-being.

The boat is mostly blue, the decking mostly green, the chairs a pale yellow. The table is decorated with turquoise flowers. There are, within the flowers, red berries. Within the berries are black seeds. There was a rug we once had, in the early days, that was the same colour as the dress Bev's wearing now. A dirty orange. The light is doing something ghostly; her dress, her unsunned skin, her graying hair, all seem to be dissolving. The light is glitzing, playing tricks. With Poole it's all different. His bright red jumper and chocolate skin stand out as if illuminated. His hair is worn in short dreadlocks, he has a week's growth of beard.

Suddenly, over his left shoulder, a flashing wheel appears. Seven cyclists in bright lycra rush the tow path, leaving a shower of sprayed gravel, pink and fluorescent yellow stripes around their shoulders. Old ladies and small dogs leap to safety; birds vacate the trees. Ducks submerge. Bev and Poole barely raise an eyelid. I too am unmoved; I grip the rudder and feel the depths of the canal, the silt, the mud, the gooey depths, the run and blood of the earth. I push the rudder right. Poole is mumbling something I can't make out. More space travel and celestial pathways and god talk. I leave them to it. I've had enough. I'm pooped. What I want to do now is sit here and be quiet. What I want is to feel otherwise to what I once was.

6

After all that men have done to every
defenseless thing on this planet, it is time that
not just every painting, but every piece of music,
every statue, every play, every poem and book a
man creates should say only this: We are much
too horrible for this nice place. We give up.
We quit. The end!

So wrote Kurt Vonnegut.

B ev pushes her pillow closer to mine. There is
about her something of the afternoon. The
heat, the weight, the dusted warble. I can feel the
whole length of her, toes and knees, elbow, breath.
When standing she's what? Six inches shorter than
me. When laying down we seem to be the same
height. When it's like this, late at night, just us,
when the day has given her something to talk about,
she tells me in a half whisper, making the kind of
noise a nesting chicken might make. She puts her
lips two inches from my ear and says: he's a queer
fish.

I nod and stroke her leg.

She rubs her nose and sighs, rolls over and coos
at the ceiling: the question is this.

I wait for the question.

How much do we, she asks, you and I, the

two of us, at this point in our lives, want someone sleeping under our table?

One thing my father never did was read the newspapers. Nor listen to the news. At no point did we own a TV. He operated outside any knowledge of current events. What, he used to ask, has it got to do with me? How do the doings of politics, the dresses worn by movie stars, the deaths of strangers in the Middle East, impact, in any real way, my paintings?

As if a life outside his paintings was unimaginable.

He dismissed the entire project with a weary dip of his chin.

I once gave him, for his birthday, a radio. Thinking he might like, occasionally, to hear an afternoon concert. He peered at it and asked, are news casts involved? Does that happen? Do they read the news?

Infrequently, I said, but yes.

Never once, to my knowledge, was it turned on.

I'm not an innocent, my father once told me. I'm no retreater. If you think that's who I am you're sorely mistaken.

We were in the park, by the river. We had watched a woman walk past followed by a tiny dog on a gold chain. The woman, in furs and silver sandals, had turned to the dog and said, missy mumkins loves her little pupkins more than anyone ever loved anyone in the whole wide world.

It was spring and the apple blossoms were

making a nuisance of themselves. Flapping around the place like clouds of pink, damp, bugs. We weren't watching the river, we weren't eating dough-nuts, neither were we talking; we were walking at a reasonable pace; we were companionable. It was during this accustomed quiet that my father began talking.

Don't think for a moment, he said, that I'm anything like what they say I am. It's been a long time since I was the simple minded muggins they take me for. Long time since that ship sailed. I know my place. What is it they think I do all day? Do they think there's cotton wool between my ears?

We paused in front of Watkins' plaque and my father said, they think I'm a child. The Simpleton Of Mid-Wales.

After a moment he said, I do what interests me. I nodded.

There can be no other measure of a man than that. He said. If I choose to live outside their schools and fetes does that make me backward?

He fingered a loose thread at the hem of his jacket. Seldom did we hug or embrace; our affec-tion was our own and it was different. We stood in the near warmth and watched the light. After a moment he did something he had never done before and would never do again. He spoke in a barely audible whisper about his paintings. Not to me specifically, though I was included, but to the park, the trees, to his fellow painters, to the hills and rivers of his youth, to the whole bloody show.

They are, he said, about pure thingness. My objects. And the spaces between them, between us and them. About what it is to be outside, removed, isolated, away from the world.

As has been said: Ceci n'est pas une bouteille.

They call me a throwback, he said, say I belong to a different era, an earlier era, but do I not belong to my cups and saucers? The cups and saucers I buy *now*? That live *now*?

They laugh at me. They *laugh*.

Is there, he asked, anything more modern than an object removed from its purpose?

They aren't paintings at all, but ways of being with things. He said. I allow a jug to be what it is. To whomever sees it. Is not the choosing and placing of my objects a work of art in and of itself?

His eyes fell to the path beneath our feet. He toed a lump of gravel and mumbled a sentence that ended: is a plate, a cup, a salt shaker invisible? Are they to be forever neglected, ignored? Being speechless. Objects of no pressing importance…

What I'm doing, he said, what I'm attempting, in my own way, successful or not, is to paint light, heat, memory, touch. All on the surface of a cup. That's my story. Is that to be ignored? Is it? Am I to be passed over?

Bev beside me in the soupy night pushes at the blanket and sighs. Says, you got any idea what it is we're doing?

Escaping?

On a boat that, if we're lucky, travels four miles an hour?

I didn't say we're escaping quickly. We're escaping in slow motion.

As we lived. She says.

There's a dog now, on the tow path, barking. Which starts an owl hooting. Which produces, from Poole, a series of low grunts.

He hasn't got a home, says Bev. He wanders around.

In winter?

He stays with friends. On sofas, in barns, wherever.

A wanderer.

Something like that.

She puts her hand on my forehead and this is how we lay, touching, not moving, listening, waiting. The dog leaves, the owl stills, Poole settles.

There was a place, once, where we used to be outdoors. A favourite bench near a giant, concrete squirrel. It was there we sat and ate chocolate. Sometimes an apple too. When they were most in season and local and not shipped halfway around the world from some outlandish place like New Zealand. The Egremont Russet being our preferred choice, fresh from a small farm in Sussex. On the bench a silver plaque said: In Loving Memory of Laura Goode who sat here often and now sits in heaven.

Do you, I whisper, remember Beckenham Park?

I try not to. She says.

She pulls gently at a lock of my hair and says, it's best that way.

Not one to be nettled and burned by the past. She stays busy with herself; doesn't dwell on some cumbersome used to be. She lives, somehow, in the unsettled now.

Poole, she says, told me this.

It was something about biblical codes and about how if you take the third letter in every fourth word in the Book Of Lamentations, add them together and divide them by seven you come up with the name of an Egyptian king and how the letters in his name add up to the date of the first NASA moon launch.

Poole, she says, is a scholar of crypticness.

Whatever that means.

It means, she says, that he *delves*. Looks beneath.

Means he's loopy. I say.

Not, she says, that the NASA trip was the first trip to the moon. No sir. Not by a long ways. People been going on space outings for hundreds of years. The moon and beyond. Creeping round out there doing all sorts.

She's getting sleepy.

According to Poole. She says.

To which I'm silent.

Delving, she says, is to be defended. As is

loopiness. As is wandering. As are morning exercises.

As are old men, she whispers, with ulcers.

Never once, in our life together, did we travel. It was a discussion we sometimes started. Barcelona was mentioned. As were the Canary Islands. Berlin, Vienna, places of that ilk. Places we'd mostly read about. Thomas Bernhard, Michel del Castillo, Ignazio Silone, Cesare Pavese, Cadavy. That kind of company. We once went so far as to book tickets to Athens. But no, at the last minute, cancelled.

Travel, Bev said, is violence.

Not one to be uprooted and bloodied, whisked about.

The radio, she said. Our dinner plates. My students. Our hand towels.

Who could argue? What had travel to offer me? New smells I suppose. New ways to be uncomfortable.

Why should the world, asked Bev, be our playground? What have we done to deserve that?

So off we bussed to Sussex. Weekends here and there. In all the damp pubs around Rye, East Ditchling, Lewes. Sometimes across to Hastings. The South Downs and all that. And of course there was always damp Wales, to see my father.

Being away from London, between hedgerows, was travel enough. Amongst birds and unleashed dogs, plants we didn't know the names of, lanes that graveled into farm yards. Where there were morning chickens. We walked a great deal and, by the evening, listening to the radio, fell asleep early.

In those days I knew how. Sleep came unasked. We were different then.

Abulia: lack of will or motivation, usually manifested as an inability to make decisions or set goals. Abulic: the adjective form of abulia.

I long ago settled into an abulic trance.

Sometimes I feel sorry but mostly I don't think about it; it's me. It's not a terrible way to be. Sometimes at night, in Camberwell with the curtains drawn, when the moon was out there, I suspected that maybe I was born with weak blood. Never diagnosed. And that I'd been living with a terminal weakness my entire life. What about that? Possible. I certainly wasn't the child who exhausted people with my antics. I sat quietly and kept to myself. Walking long distances wearied me. I never ran or played sports. I had a bicycle that I rarely pedaled; I learned to mostly coast around. Even as a grown up fella, cycling across the river with Bev, she would shout: come on slow coach, get a move on!

I've been, always, three or four steps behind the world.

Damn but don't we all get old. Unrecognizable in our saggings and discolourings. Where once we looked like who we were, now we look like all old things; chipped and frail and immobile. We join, in old age, nature. Exposed rock, mossy bark, wind kneeled trees, flattened fields, stagnant ponds.

Ric, I'm told, died from cancer in the liver. There was kidney trouble too and his properties, what few remained, had been taken from him. Involved, as he was, in an ongoing dispute with the tax man.

7

I realize that the lack, in these pages, of a mother, of my mother, might seem strange. It's not something I dwell on. There are stranger things. For instance: the national animal of Scotland is the unicorn. The national animal of Wales is the dragon. The national animal of England is the lion. Two fictional beasts and one that has never been native to these parts.

As concerns my mother, or the woman who birthed me and was very much not my mother, my father once said: you're not to hate her. One mustn't hate what one doesn't know.

He treated the entire affair as he treated most things; detached, impassive, wondering. He spoke of it as one might speak of an explosion or a traffic accident; something witnessed but not understood.

We were married, he said, and she fell pregnant and when you were born she came to me and said: I've made a terrible mistake.

It was that simple. *A terrible mistake.*

People make mistakes. He said.

She was brave enough, he said, to be honest.

She left and I stayed and my father never spoke ill of her. He trusted me to understand; the mistake was marriage, himself, pregnancy, the maze of adulthood; not me.

I began to understand then that my father thought almost exclusively in pictures. Pictures being the way he organized the world. Not words, not letters, not numbers, not ideas. Action didn't enter into it. He inhabited a world of images. First this one and then the next. Each one separate, not commenting on or canceling out the next. They simply gave way. You neither judged nor excused them. You viewed them, at a remove. He saw, each morning, the picture of his breakfast, not the process. He saw his toast and marmalade; not his hunger, not the cost, not the taste, not the nutritional benefits, not the act of eating.

The same with his wife. He saw a picture of her busy at her deeds, not her desires, her disappointments, her pleasures, her sorrows. And when she left he saw a different space arranged in a different way. Two pictures, one not necessarily better than the other.

Do you, Bev once asked, want to find her? Meet her?

No, no, no, no, no, I said. And again no.

Really?

It's a complication. I said.

Complications being, for me, endless.

One more thing I didn't need.

Bev made a face and went quiet. A shadow sat upon her nose. At which point I felt a great wave of devotion for her. I gripped her hand and felt awful. She was, at that moment, everything in the world to me. Which left me thinking: how does a man ever get to the root of that rootless thing, that omnivorous outing called attraction.

8

Thin men have curious yearnings.

So wrote Warren Miller.

Poole's talking. He's washed himself and has managed, somehow, to smell of coconuts. He's looking across the canal and telling us that he never asked to be a part of this planet, but here he is, so anything he does here is because the Creator of the Universe is telling him to do it.

I'm from out there, he says, from another dimension. I'm a psychic being - I don't concern myself with being born; with the whys and where-fores of all that, I'm concerned with being eternal; I deal with the bigger picture. And I'm telling you that somewhere on the other side of nowhere is a place beyond time where the Gods of mythology dwell in their mythocracies as opposed to your theocracies, democracies, and monocracies. They dwell in a magic world. In their world you just 'think' the place you want to go and your mind will take you there.

And then: at first there was nothing and then nothing turned itself inside-out and became something.

For the first time in a couple of weeks it rains. We take refuge inside, below deck, on the same level as the water. Rain does its plop, plop, platter. The day closes. I don't mind. I've always been the kind that likes a rainy world.

How seriously we sit here.

The rain does both little things and big things. It flushes down and wets things but doesn't clean them. It compacts the world; the edges are muddled. The sky which is usually very high and distant and far away is made lower, still too high to touch but less lofty. The rain takes the place of air; we become gilled creatures, scaled and finned.

How seriously we sip our tea. We have, it would seem, no responsibilities. Only to fill the space between ourselves with words. Poole talks, Bev talks, I talk. Mostly Bev and I nod and agree. We say little things and we say them quietly. Poole expands. It's nice to sit this way, listening to things I don't really understand. I do my best but my best wanders. It's more the sound of Poole that I like than the meaning. I like the swag and lilt of it, like listening to Sonny Rollins or Rashaan Roland Kirk. I think maybe the important thing about language is how it sounds, not what it means. As the important thing about travel is its unfoldingness. There are tiny, not quiet stabs of rain all around. Where do the ducks and bugs and small birds go when it rains? Is there a secret room somewhere where they gather, sitting around like Bev and Poole and

I are here, mumbling and story telling, comparing grievances, killing time, each of them listening but not really paying attention.

Bev and I had, for a time, let's say nine years ago, a neighbor by the name of Davis. It might have been either his first or surname, I never knew. He was always just Davis. He was of the kind that wishes to please. A smiling fella somewhere in his middle age. He had both a caged bird and a dog, the dog being a toy poodle, the bird being something small and green. He regularly took them out when he visited Camberwell Green. The three would sit on a bench; man, dog, bird. Was it a parakeet? Or budgerigar? It's name was Mr. Thomas; it whistled incessantly. The dog was called Westy. Most evenings, weather permitting, on my arrival home from McPherson's, I saw them there, Davis, Westy and Mr. Thomas.

Davis often hung himself with bright necklaces. His wardrobe was pleasingly pitched somewhere between athletic wear and more feminine touches, including lipstick, rouge, eyeliner and flowery scarves. Sometimes, but not always, high heels. He was a man who wore a little of this and a little of that. His hair was carefully piled. He always had a nice word to say. I thought, but was never sure, that there might be a foreign accent involved. They seemed a happy family. He was the only person I've ever known who called Bev Beverly. When I came off the bus, on my way home, and saw the three of them there, sitting in a row on their bench, he always waved and gave his shoulders a shake. Sometimes he'd say, Westy's feeling ever so slightly sluggish today. Or, Mr. Thomas is enjoying a premium mix of pumpkin and sunflower seeds. Or sometimes, if he had nothing he wanted to say, he waved and shook his necklaces and left it at that. I liked the way the three of them looked and I asked Bev about maybe getting a dog or cat but she always said the same thing: the two of us get along just fine. We know who we are. Another body, furred or otherwise, might upset things.

I agreed and so we lived alone, just the two of us.

When the rain lets up the day goes silky. If silky means thin and somehow translucent, everything flowing into everything else. What we do is we listen to birds returning. There's one, with a red wedge on its head, that comes tilting over the water. On the towpath two rabbits are doing what rabbits do.

I was just thinking, I tell Bev, about Davis.

She smiles and tells Poole: he called me Beverly.

Poole rotates his shoulders.

Mr. Thomas, she says, was a dear little fella.

She imitates Poole, rotating her shoulders.

Not, she says, that I approved of the cage.

They get up and begin their exercises, folding left and right. Poole, taking charge, counts to twenty. He's large and Bev isn't. I walk to the rear of the boat and stand watching the water. My ulcer isn't doing much. I feel washed out in a not unpleasant way. A stiff breeze would lay me low. Leaves and twigs are doing some floating. As, of course, are we.

Might there be fish below or birds above that, like me, have torn stomachs? That have been unable to find their place in the world? Are there rabbits or squirrels that look upon the world and are defeated? I doubt it. Birds fly, rabbits burrow, fish swim - until they don't. They are and then they aren't. Only men occupy a middle, muddy ground. I *almost* am. I *try*. I *endeavor*. Strangely, standing here, floating, neither coming nor going, moored, in the not too warm day, with my weak blood doing its inching, I feel more certain of my place in the world than I ever have. I'm *here*. With Bev. Away from *there*. Where a constant tumult of things were always happening and then, instantly, rehappening. Things too loud and terribly sure of themselves. I'm here now where things put on less of a show. One thing happens and then something else happens and there's enough time between the two things to let them sink in and take hold and mean something.

The flight of a bird is an event that has its own meaning. An unlanguaged and nontransferable meaning. It has meaning precisely because, to us, it's meaningless.

Fish too and bugs and the constant life of a

hedgerow. They have a meaning outside the world of our meaning.

Bev is the yolk of my world.

Shall we? I hear her say and the deck beneath my feet shifts. Slowly we're cast off. We float for a moment before the engine starts. Poole has the rudder. We lean west, moving just enough to call it moving. I hear some discussions in the back and make my way there. There's a lock coming up, says Bev.

Half an hour. Says Poole.

I nod and add nothing. Not being much of an adder.

I make a motion as if I'm sipping tea and Bev says, oh yes please.

Poole nods and says, lovely.

So it's down to the kitchen I go. We have, in the cupboard, three cartons of tea bags. We have powdered milk and two cartons of soya milk. We have food for weeks. Tofu and rice, beans and ginger, spaghetti, tins of tomatoes, dried beans and assorted veg. We have oil and vinegar. We have books and clean socks. We have pillow cases and blankets. We have what we could carry. Bev has her cello, I have my ulcer.

We have, as well, money. Not endless but enough. For fifty years we've lived discreetly, some might say we barely lived at all. Our rent was minimal. Most of what I made at McPherson's, minus Ric's rent, I banked. Bev did the same with her cello lessons. We seldom went out, didn't travel, had no children. The sale of my father's house brought an early deposit. We neither planned nor hoped. We sought no financial advice. We lived as we lived and when the time came to leave we had a small pile in the bank.

Lucky us.

Now we have this. This boat and what fits therein.

I had, for fifty years, three paintings of my father's. One I sold, one I gave away, one I've kept. The sold painting (to an Italian collector), along with a chunk of our savings, paid for this boat. It was a painting of a fork, a spoon, an egg cup and a bread knife. I rescued it from the rubbish when I was twenty. I told my father that I both liked and wanted it. He looked at it, shook his head sadly and said: the spoon got away from me. It's...it's just a spoon. Any spoon. Not the spoon I was painting.

The objects were arranged on a dull, pinkish, grey table. A table I knew well. One of three tables on which my father placed his objects. The painting hung, for years, in Bev's and my Camberwell kitchen.

The painting I have left now hangs above our bed. It was started the week I was born and given to me on my fifteenth birthday. It contains, unusually, only one object, a bowl. The bowl from which

I ate my morning cereal. I would use no other; it was my bowl. It is, I think, one of my father's finest paintings. Everything about it just right. A dull green table, a yellow light, an off white bowl with a single blue stripe around it's rim. He never tried to sell it; it hung first in his studio and then in my bedroom.

And now on this boat.

We were absolutely not clever. When were we ever clever? We bought the first boat we saw. It appeared well maintained, the paintwork was new, there were potted plants on the deck, the engine quiet, it had a fitted kitchen and a double bed. The seller wanted a quick sale; the harbor master said it was a right tidy boat; we handed over the most money we'd ever handed over in our lives. The deal done.

We knew nothing about narrow boats or canals. We knew almost nothing about anything. We were ill prepared. We read a few books. We asked questions. We trusted. We did as a million before us have done: we leapt. We knew only that we wanted out. And a narrow boat, going three miles an hour, seemed our speed. We left from Little Venice in west London and drifted north. We learned as we went. Or we learned enough. Or we appeared to learn something. Mostly we did what we saw other people doing. We became mimickers.

A sudden uproar of wind sweeps across the deck; I

look to the rear of the boat and see Poole's dread-locks standing on end. On the towpath a small sign indicating the upcoming lock clatters. I take a seat, blown about and dizzy. I pull my jumper up around my neck and the drama passes. Bev and Poole, their hair all wind slapped, join me in my sprawl.

Whattagust! Says Poole.

His eyes are shining, as if they've just seen some-thing unpronounceable. Bev puts her hand on my arm and gives me a How You Doing look.

I'm fine, I say.

Her fingers tighten and I can feel a tender qualm in her grip.

Really. I say.

She leans in and I can smell her. Her cardigan the colour of mistletoe. Her lips brush my forehead and what she whispers is, Mouse.

There were days when no one came. No mumblers, no silencers, no time wasters, no conspirators. Only me, there, behind my makeshift counter. In my raggedy jumper and flannel trousers. I had my box of change and McPherson's chair. My beret. I wasn't uncomfortable. I kept the lights low. Two basement rooms full of nothing. On these days I pleased myself. A roll of biscuits, cups of tea, push back my chair, turn up the music.

On these days I made believe.

I hankered for things like familiarity and com-fort and grace and ease.

I let the music hammer me and knock me around, I let it do what it had in its mind to do, I got split up and wounded, I got relieved, I needed that intervention, that wonderfulness; sometimes I floated around and felt weightless and was genuinely lost and there were moments when I looked down on myself and McPherson's from a great and fearful height.

There were moments, when listening to Gary Bartz or The Art Ensemble Of Chicago, that I ceased to be me. Whatever that was. I felt bodiless and mindless. Not a significant part of my own life. At all other times I felt locked into an oppressive need to justify and understand and define. During those basement days I was some other type of person. Closer, I think, to someone like my father. I was settled into the flimsy now, the present.

Music wasn't a noun, it was a verb. I was involved in a way mysterious to me. I was *in there*. Have you ever heard Clifford Jordan's In The World on Strata-East Records? Or Sweet Earth Flying by Marion Brown? Or Spirit Dance by Michael White? These records rained through me, lashing, puddling here and there. They left me bruised and different. I was thankful to them and told them so.

Music, that kind of music, music of that nature, can make the lights come on.

The moon, says Poole, is a celestial magnet. A million years ago it was part of a bigger, super magnet that was split apart by God. God can do that. God does whatever God wants to do. The pieces of the magnet were spread around the universe in order to attract life forms. God keeps track of where the magnets are. God knows. He knows that the moon attracted the earth. He's aware of us and what we think we're doing. The moon is the centre of things, the puller. The moon is doing God's bidding. That's why, at night, if it's a clear, it's impossible not to look at the moon. It's calling us.

Poole continues in this extraterrestrial vein until the lock is nearly upon us.

It's time. I say.

Gentlemen assume your positions. Says Bev.

Poole rudders us over and turns off the engine. We knock against the canal wall as Bev climbs off the boat, carrying the lock opening gear turner thing. Which I'm sure has a proper name. Which I should know but don't. As I said; we're beginners. Bev crosses the canal on the narrow gangway on top of the lock. Her legs, her arms, her feet and hands; all quick as a squirrel. On the other side she cranks the lock gates open and the water in the lock rises. When it reaches the same level as the canal Poole slowly moves the boat forward. When we're in Bev closes the lock doors, secures them, crosses back over, and runs to the next lock. The process is repeated and we wait for the water level in the lock to lower. The boat lowers with it. As does Poole. As do I. As does all our stuff. We sink until we're the same level as the next section of the canal. At which point we move forward and Bev closes the gates.

This is the way things work on the canal. Forward slowly, stop, moor, forward, lock, moor, forward, stop, lock. It's a pace that demands reflection. Contemplation. Bookishness. Quietude. All the locked away monk type behavior. The behavior that is not common human endeavour.

I take the rudder while Bev and Poole arrange themselves on the bow. I can't hear what's being said. I don't want to. It's another layer of noise; water, wind, birds, engine, leaves; all of it puffing and whirring.

We drift. Gradually.

As do my thoughts and my blood. As do ducks and bugs. As will Poole come winter. Drifters all.

In this way, this dawdling and methodical way, we proceed. This way that has more to do with shadow-making than with propulsion; more to do with hush and barrenness than purpose; more painstaking than intentioned.

9

What am I that the sun and the mountains
and the lake are not? What is expected of me
that is not expected of them?

So wrote Kenneth Patchen.

I remember sitting with Fritz, my father's agent, in his kitchen. It was the most beautiful kitchen I'd ever seen. Bev's and my entire flat would have easily fit inside it. The floor was oak, 200 years old; the boards were twelve inches wide. We sat on Georgian chairs that were elegant without being showy. There were twelve of them. He served Earl Grey tea with lemon.

People, he said, are indefensible, people are just awful. The indefensible awfulness of people goes without saying. There can be no arguments in this regard. This is a fact.

I stirred my tea.

Why isn't this commonly acknowledged? Why doesn't everyone know this? Why is this not taught in schools? Why, in this day and age, is this not taken for granted? He asked.

Fritz was four years older than me. There had been, recently, an article in a national paper that called him "an engaging if somewhat unpleasant man". I had never found him unpleasant; he doted on me, flirted, flattered me with his attentions.

He'd given up his office and now worked from home. He camped amongst a worrying clutter of canvasses, frames, scrolls, portfolios, boxes, stacks of paper. He came from immense and unhappy wealth. He threw around baskets of money; he made and lost it, it meant something different to him than it did to me. It was his curse. He seemed to exceed the space he occupied. His skin having a translucent paleness, his hair being the white of a rat's belly. He was without cunning, a man of dense but regrettable honour.

He pulled, from a stack of paintings, one by my father and said, I wept when I saw this. Wept. Like a little girl. Wept like a baby.

I didn't doubt it. I'd seen him cry on numerous occasions. He was a weeper.

He held the canvas at arms length and was silent. Finally his head shook and his arm fell and he said, how many among us can do that? Eh? How bloody many?

They'd been introduced at a gallery; Fritz had said to my father, there are three great painters left in the world and you're one of them.

My father, embarrassed and pleased, said nothing. Fritz was, at the time, thirty-four years old, a dandy, gorgeous, born of misgivings. He hovered and he insisted.

You need two things, he told my father. You need an agent and you need me.

Again, from my father, silence. He tried something with his mouth that he imagined was a smile. It wasn't. Two months later Fritz got his way; he began the unenviable task of selling my father's pictures.

He failed.

My father wasn't displeased. He expected failure. There was no displeasure in him. For Fritz it was a scandal.

The public, he said, are wholly loathsome.

Fritz wore pink striped jackets and tartan trousers. He wore cravats of an oriental origin. His shoes were hand-made; a cast of each foot was kept on file. His shirts came from India, his under garments were bought in bulk and worn only once. He had a body spray specially made from calendula, baby bay leaves, single malt and Spanish lavender.

I am, he once said, too vile to be voiced.

He was weeping at the time.

Mankind, he said, holding my father's painting, is not to be commended. We had our chance and we blew it. We caved in and we got ugly. We said yes to all the bad stuff.

He put down the picture and held up his hands in a mea culpa poise.

Me, he said, I was at the front of the queue. That's where I was. Front and bloody centre. When they were handing out greed and pettiness and a life long supply of avarice. I admit it. I was right there with my hand out. But at least I was a child. I was doing what children do – push to the front and take more than their fair share of whatever's going. It was all about me. Me and whatever I thought was important. Which was basically anything that made my life easier and more dramatic and fuller of shiny nonsense than it already was.

He worked with my father for the rest of my father's life; he finally managed to sell a few paintings at greatly increased prices. My father's routine never shifted, he silenced and he pondered and he mulled and he reflected. While Fritz swooned and was generally tireless; his life being one of constant schooling, soirees, personal cultural betterment, refinement, purity, elegance, that sort of caper.

He replaced my father's painting in its stack and said, what we're seeing, what we're witnessing, what we western fortunates are eyeballing is this. The end days. The Roman days of ruination and collapse.

There was, on the wall behind him, a painting by Evelyn Dunbar. To his left was an engraving by Clare Leighton. There were somewhere, I knew, paintings by Gwen Johns and Winifred Nicholson. His wardrobe still featured over tailored suits; he still wept. His house was choked with art.

Have you, he asked, given it any thought? The

thing I asked you.

I had. A great deal of thought.

The thing that had happened, a month previous, at a small gallery on Cork Street, was this: Fritz had liquored himself, pushed me into a corner and done some talking. What he said was: leave Bev and be with me. Live with me. Come be with me and it'll be like whatever good thing you can imagine. It'll be like that. It'll be like that but even better.

There were small splashes of something on his shoes. And his hair was not in a good place. True, he smelled lovely and his waistcoat was impressive, but on balance he was not, I repeat not, in a good place. He got like that when he drank, sort of shoved around and panicked.

Have you read Maurice, he asked, by Forester? Those last ten pages when everything is decided?

He breathed heavily on me and said, does that appeal?

I did what my father had taught me to do. I did nothing. Said nothing. My face and I gave nothing away.

Well? He asked.

I stood for entire minutes while he told me how it would be for us. I got the feeling he was mostly quoting Forester. Like he was repeating something he wanted to be true. There was a lot about how we were going to go to Italy, just the two of us, the two of us and his money, and be away from all the stuff we were currently being stifled by.

I looked over his shoulder at a roomful of wealthy people doing those things that those people have always done at those events. I hadn't wanted to come; Fritz had insisted.

I'm getting older. He said. *We're* getting older.

He wasn't wrong. He wasn't often wrong. He was in possession of ample facts. He knew a lot about a lot of things. He'd been bred that way. He'd taken his opportunities. He was intrepid and sudden and he didn't much care what people thought. He was, in the way of large men who move well, admirable. I admired him.

My father, a year before he died, had been asked to give a talk at the Institute For Contemporary Arts. They were presenting a week of lectures exploring the relationship between painting, solitariness, outsiders and contemplation.

It'll put you in the company of O'Keefe, Morandi, Hopper and Braque, Fritz told him. Right there with Russian icon painters and Giacometti and Alfred Wallis.

I don't want company, my father had said. That's the point, people like me, if there are any other people like me, we don't want company.

You won't be interrupted, Fritz said. You won't have to answer questions. The night is yours.

I can't, my father whispered. I just can't. I never could.

Fritz must have suspected as much; he had a lecture of his own prepared. He took the podium in my father's place, (wearing a muted suit of salmon pink) and delivered a paper entitled How Awful We Are And How Shallow.

He looked out across the gathered glitterati and said, you have ruined things.

His voice was stiff with warning, biting hard on his consonants. He'd tried to shape his hair; it had the look of a flower arrangement. The audience, made up almost entirely of his friends, clients and colleagues, said not a word. He glowered.

With your manners, your politeness, your pension plans, your savings, your movies, your restaurants, your children. Your pleasantries. Your mean little phones. We must, he said, accept responsibility for what we've done.

The crowd stirred. And exhaled. They sat upright in their chairs. And leaned ever so slightly forward. Fritz outlined a hundred years of meanness, of petty mindedness, of money pillaging around the place. It wasn't a pretty picture.

Where did we go? He asked. How did we get there? Who are we now that we've arrived?

He walked from one end of the stage to the other, performing two tight little turns at either end. This, he said, is our failure. This is the story of our lives. This is the failure not of politics or family or economics, but of the imagination. A failure of beauty. A failure of incredulity. Once we believed that we were worth believing in. We believed in the stories we invented. We believed in tall tales. We spun fictions that were bigger than the world. That *were* the world. Now, well –

He stamped his expensively shod foot.

– we only believe in what we own, what we make, what we want, what we possess. What we can buy and keep. Science, accumulation, maintenance, money. We no longer believe that art, the product of us, poor lost naked children, is worth believing in. And when imagination is forgotten, the unimaginable becomes real. The unimaginable becomes all there is.

When, he asked, did art become just another investment opportunity?

Fritz was the one who had thrown this little quote at me: *Without music life would be a mistake –* Frederick Nietzsche.

I had, for a moment, agreed. As I almost always agreed with him. As was my way. Agree and keep quiet. He'd been drinking and had, that afternoon, sold a painting he disliked for more money than he thought it worth. He'd doubled his investment. The check was on his desk. There were a lot of zeros involved. He'd wept a little and said, no. Even *with* music, with art, with poetry, with port, with wine, *still* a mistake. Always a mistake. Life is a mistake. A mistake we keep on making.

At which point I stood, collected my coat and

scarf, and said, well, well.

Well, well?

I looked at him with an uncertain fondness. Above the fire place hung a self portrait by William Roberts. To its left was a drawing by Eric Gill. Below that, reaching almost to the floor, was a medieval map of Britain, with sea monsters on every coast. On the table was a vase by Lucie Rea.

The life of an azalea or the life of a goat is not a mistake. I said. Nor the life of a rock. Nor a forest. Only men make mistakes.

I looped my scarf around my neck and said, and continue making them.

On, slowly, went my duffle coat. Of an undistinguished colour, tartan lining and wooden toggles.

Bev, I said, is waiting.

I need, whispered Fritz, to unravel. A little. I need to get uncivilized. A little. I need to be loosened.

He took my hand, turned it and kissed the palm. He was a figure of true gravity. Never did his zeal diminish; it was to him, a year later, that I gave the third of my father's paintings.

The painting was entitled Group S27. My father named paintings in gatherings and tribes that were evident to him and no one else. He refused to elaborate. They are named, he said, and that's the end of it.

The painting was small, ten inches by twelve

inches, and contained two items, a shaving brush and a box of matches. Fritz had cried on receipt of it, saying, I am fatigued with pleasure.

He crossed the room, removed from its place between two windows a drawing by Arthur Kitching, and replaced it with Group S27.

He stood back and was, for a moment, pleased. I hoped he was. He had that air. There was a way he tilted his head. There were no words, just a small, sighing gurgle. A death rattle. Finally he turned, his velvet slippers hissing on the carpet, and said, let us consider two words.

I waited.

Anamnesis and epitasis.

I waited.

The first being Greek and meaning the loss of forgetfulness. He said. The second referring to that part of a play that develops the main action but leads directly to the catastrophe. These two words describe exactly where we are today.

He often spoke that way during moments of complexity, like a teacher or a priest, a social worker, like someone in charge of small children. Sounding rather like the actor Charles Laughton.

I read both words recently, he said, in a book that, for a few minutes anyway, broke me of all my dull habits.

When I returned home I told Bev what Fritz had said. Italy, he and I, Forester, Maurice, our future happiness, everything.

Poor Fritz. She said.

I agreed.

Did you, she asked, say something nice?

I told her that I had said nothing.

Oh. She said. Poor Fritz.

What could I say? I asked.

Bev looked at me with what I guess you'd call pity and said nothing. Then shook her head and said, people talk. Most people. They use their words. That's what they do. They say some little thing, a couple sentences, they remind whoever it is they're with that they're both there, in the same room. They take an interest. You might have thanked him for the offer and said that while you were unable to accept there are many things in this world you could have learned from him. You might have told him he's a good man.

The light in our kitchen wasn't golden, it wasn't comforting; Bev shook her head again and said, he was good to your father. He's been good to you.

Her lips narrowed. Mouse, she said, you're a puzzle.

I agreed. And tried to think of something to say. I tried for a full five minutes. I stood in the unconsoling night and watched moths at the window. Nothing came to mind.

10

The mind that is not baffled is not employed.
The impeded stream is the one that sings.

So wrote Wendell Berry.

This is Poole: there was an explosion, a divine explosion, an explosion that had no origin, and it set the universe on fire. The flames were made of black ice. We were born of fire. We were exploded. We were burnt and blasted and we were made into this.

He grips his own arm and says, flesh.

First there was an hour about Atlantis, its demise and its continuing role in the mysterious aquatic life of the Atlantic; then it was ancient English history and the story of Danish invasions; then we had something about the Free Masons and Catholic sects and how the pope is the direct descendent of Guillaume le Batard, aka William the Bastard, aka William the Conqueror; now, finally, we're on the explosive origins of mankind.

He isn't really talking to us, he's talking to the world, reminding it if his being, staking his claim, marking his territory. Telling it: I have words and I exist. Bev has finished listening, she's half in, half out of the sun, reading. She's wearing her ridiculous hat and huge sunglasses, of the kind often sold to children, red rims and blue glass. Her ankles as trim as cotton spools.

This millennial business is upon us. Says Poole. We are both doomed and bewitched.

He's talking about celestial portals, historical epochs, intersections of collapse.

The coming age, he says, will be one of reversal.

His voice ratchets up a notch and he says, what once was small shall be big, the mighty shall be weak, the prosperous will falter, the solid will become like air. We will kneel.

Not once does Bev look up.

Exhausted, I go below deck and lay down.

We are nothing but trouble. We can all, I hope, agree on that. My friend the doctor, in his lifeless office, looking to reassure me, said: our bodies produce two hundred billion red blood cells every day. They churn out hemoglobin and plasma like there's no tomorrow. Our bodies, he said, know what they're doing.

We produce, the good doctor said, 40,000 litres of urine over the course of a lifetime. We grow twenty-eight meters of finger nails and shed nineteen kilos of dead skin.

He said this in the same way that people stand on street corners, reminding us of life eternal and what a friend we have in Jesus. His eyes bright.

I was not reassured. I was not made glad. I was

fretful. What I was was uneasy.

What we do, I said, is we increase. We extinguish. We run riot. We don't stop.

I sat in his steel and yellow leather chair and felt buried. There was, I felt, something about my body, on a skeletomuscular level, that was dissolving. I was experiencing a discontinuity in which sweat was involved and a bloating, a realignment. I slouched back.

We have, I told him, over the past forty years, killed off over a quarter of all living things with whom we share this planet. With our overwhelmingness. All. Living. Things. Around and below and above us. A quarter of all living things that will never be living again. 25 per cent of all those who lived on land. 33 per cent of those who swam. 22 per cent of those who flew. That didn't swim fast or fly high enough to get away from us. A quarter of all arctic life. More acres of rain forest than we can measure.

The good doctor said, a terrible sin yes, but not *your* sin.

Seeking, somehow, to excuse me from my species.

He gave me a medicinal look. He folded his hands. There was a clock on the wall that was made to look old. There were no bugs, no flies, nothing small and irritating. There was something shameful happening, a tricky, many cornered moment. Shameful in its need, its insistence. The light, on a dimmer switch, was discreet. The good doctor breathed a sound that, given the circumstance, was either seductive or heartening. It was in this amassing calm that the vision of a boat first entered my mind.

I told Bev and she didn't blink. Never was Bev a blinker. She was a doer. She began, that very night, to reduce. Boxing and throwing and giving away. In as clear headed a manner as possible. The shelves and closets were stripped. She surrounded herself with piles of this and that, debris, artifacts, mostly junk. We were quickly lessened.

I sold, with only an intermittent pang, my records to a man named Marcus. His name was passed to me by Derrick. I met Derrick through Linda. Linda lived next door to McPherson's. Linda introduced me to Alan. Alan had a shop called Basement Jazz. It was Alan who recommended Derrick.

There were, about Marcus, careless elements; he made no effort to disguise his boredom; he fidgeted; his hair was over cut; he lived in Camden. He flipped slowly through my records.

Good stuff. He said.

I knew that.

You wanna sell the lot or what?

The lot. I said.

Five hundred records that I had decided I could live without. I had, for forty years, been someone I was now trying not to be. I'm buying a boat. I said.

He wasn't interested.

A boat, I repeated.

I wanted him to know. It was important that he knew who he was dealing with. Selling up, I said.

I think there was a grunt. I couldn't be sure. There was plenty I could have said. I could have expanded, done some storytelling. Shared the loosenings and whispers of my life. The moment was there until it passed.

He pulled out a couple of Sun Ra records and said, big money.

The dust that day was everywhere evident, in little funnels and flat clouds, in the light that ribboned across the room; it grimed my skin. Sirens were hurtling around and the pace of things was faster than it needed to be. The city persisted.

My boat, I said, is twenty eight feet long.

Marcus nodded, put down the records and said, I'll take the lot.

When it's later Poole is telling us: for thirty years I was a speck, a cinder. Who cared about me? The city was a book, one of those huge books, million bloody pages and I was a comma. Not even that. I lived there until I couldn't breathe. I woke up one morning and there wasn't any air left in the world.

He gives us the blank stare and says, that's when I realized a man needs to breathe. Needs to fill his lungs.

Bev gives him a nod.

I was a bus driver. He says. Twenty eight years. Twenty eight years driving in circles every day.

His shoulders rise and fall. His neck is surprisingly delicate. He swivels around, almost like an owl, and says, the thing that saved me was that I started spending my Sundays in Knole Park, in Kent, down by Sevenoaks. You know it? They got some kind of big house there, gardens and whatever, Vita Sackville used to live there, and they got more acres than God's got and you can walk around and look at the trees or whatever, have a picnic, listen to the birds go about their business, but mostly, what I did, what I got really into, was looking at the deer.

I dip my head a couple times. Knole Park I know. There's a picture of my fathers' in the big house. Three eggs on a blue plate. Or so I've been told, so it says in some book; I've never seen it.

I wanted, says Poole, a place where I could breathe. Where I could say here I am and it's OK to be here and no one's gonna make me leave. I took to following those deer around all day. Miles and miles. Rain and sun. Had some kind of slow breakdown. A suspension of who I was. Began, for the first time, to miss days at work. Took sick days. Went down to the deer every chance I could. Stopped looking after the little things. Laundry got erratic. Passengers made some complaints and my supervisor filed a warning. I was becoming a different kind of person and I didn't know who. The deer became the only real thing in my life. I think, I guess, that maybe, in some corner of my mind, I joined them. The herd. I got into what I thought was the head of a deer.

Confusing. He says. A confusing time.

His shoulders heave and he closes his eyes. Runs his hand across his forehead and through his dreadlocks. Says, long story short I got lost. Real lost. No job, no flat, no way to get back into a world I didn't want to be in in the first place.

He sips some tea, Bev sips some tea, I sip some tea. All of us sipping tea, intent on different possibilities. I can feel my blood stalled around my stomach. I need to get up, shake things around a little.

I drank, says Poole. A lot. For a while. When they banned me from the park I did some other stuff too. Dumb stuff. Bottomed out. Bad stuff. Lost touch with who I was. Ceased, really, to be anything. Just drifted around. Just trash on the street. The stuff that collects in doorways.

He arches his eyebrows and whistles.

Poole, he says, got punished.

When I was a boy, after breakfast, after washing up my bowl and cleaning away my cereal, my father would ask me the same question: may I walk with you to school?

He was sincere; he was seeking my permission. Usually I was happy to say yes. We would leave the house walking slowly, my father with his hands in his pockets, smelling slightly of oil and turpentine. The school was a small brick building on the edge of the village. A ten minute walk. There were oak trees and willows and sheep behind fences and, occasionally, cats the colour of smoke that would streak across the road. There were some but not many cars. In the winter the trees were bare and the birds were gone and the cats stayed indoors. Sometimes we passed groups of children that looked at me but said nothing. I wasn't part of their games. They lived their lives without me. My father might point out a single red leaf or a fallen button or a scrap of paper.

Well, well, he'd say, look at that.

His way of walking, formal and upright, shoulders loose, fully aware, had a density that seemed to rule out missteps. He connected with the pavement in a direct and meaningful way. Years later, watching an evening of modern dance, I watched Merce Cunningham cross the stage with a similar purposefullness.

Bev brings some rice cakes and peanut butter to the table. A plate too of cucumber and celery and spinach leaves. She pushes the plate across to me and I don't say thank you. I nod and touch her arm. Poole is standing at the rudder, watching the canal.

Bev sits and picks up her book. She spreads her fingers across the black and white cover. I watch their nails and knuckles. Hands that play Shubert and Feldman and Cage and Bach. Hands that have aged and not aged, that are sure and not sure. That have been denied. The word that comes to mind is misgivings.

How can I, at this point, make amends?

We slept, for the first five years of our marriage, on the floor. We often ate noodles for breakfast. Our sofa, our table, were street finds. We opted, always, for the cheap seats. Our way of being now seems not to be the consequence of our life then. To be honest, we got lucky. Little about us is the result of my efforts. Bev is a beauty and I'm not and she's good hearted and I'm forgetful. And now tired. There is nothing in the world I deserve.

There were things about being the way we were that neither of us liked. We lived with meager disappointments, with great solitariness. We dismantled and were sometimes provisional; we accepted; we did what we did. We were alive for years.

Bev says that what we feel is less important than how we feel it.

11

When you travel your first discovery
is that you do not exist.

So wrote Elizabeth Hardwick.

The rememberer and the remembered; the fish, the pig; the truck, the fire; the song, the singer; the buyer and the bought; all short lived. There are oak trees that survive 1000 years; I've seen them, stood near them; rivers, oceans, mountains, all the earth stuff that carry on regardless.

Fritz came to see us off. A farewell party of one. He brought baskets of gifts. Chocolates and champagne and fancy mustard and preserved lemons in oil. Two cashmere blankets, a mahogany handled umbrella, a book about birds, scented candles, a radio. He cried. He hugged us both and made a fuss and took pictures. He made us promise to call at least once a week. Any time, he said. He stood on the side of the canal as we slowly left the quay. He'd come dressed in what he thought was an appropriate outfit, as if he was venturing with us into the wilds; a khaki suit and boots. The next day, when I opened the Book Of British Birds, fifty pound notes fluttered down from its pages.

At no point, during no days, no weeks or months, did we ever own a camera. We weren't recorders. Never did we own boxes of photos or glue pasted albums. Never did we gaze on the past in that way, through teary eyes, recollecting. We spoke, yes, occasionally we reassembled some event, saying, do you remember the time, on Westminster Bridge, we saw Howard Hodgkin on a bicycle?, but we had no camera to assist us. No black and white reminders. It was something that just never came up. Never did we hanker after a Pentax. Or a Leica. Or any other gleaming metal box. We went about our lives undocumented.

You look boiled. My doctor friend told me: I want to go on record here. What you look like is a parched carrot.

I need juice. I said. And fresh air.

He ignored me, describing the general shape and weight of my ailment, using only words that meant nothing. His imprecision, meant to be comforting, was a trick he had learnt in school.

He must have been, in his student days, a vision. Rearing and whinnying and standing with his legs wide, in a statue pose.

There are things, I said, that I happen to not like. Cars. Brussel sprouts. Polyester socks. Air travel. Wrist watches.

He drummed his fingers on his chin. He made

some impatient little movement. He said: and, among them, I suppose, people. Me, in other words.

97.5 per cent of people. I said. More or less. Let's call it 98. According to my calculations.

He launched, once again, into a description of my disorder, thinking repetition, where generalities hadn't worked, would prove soothing.

I wasn't soothed.

Am I not allowed? I asked.

Allowed?

To dislike my fellows?

Your fellows?

I said nothing.

You're allowed anything you want. He said.

He had clearly lost interest. He poured two glasses of water and gave me one. There was no other help to be given. His minty breath, his magnolia office, his sporty smile, his sun baked arms, all to no avail.

Thank you, I said.

Sitting together with our different tempers. Age is curious. The water we sipped having been flown in from France.

It doesn't, in the end, come down to any one thing. Being that there's no one thing and there's no end. This is true.

My father, near his desk, in his studio, on a filing card, had written these lines from a Wallace Stevens poem: a gold feathered bird, sings in the palm, without human meaning, without human feeling, a foreign song.

That bird was a constant fascination to me. I pictured it in some bright jungle, where the jungle meets the sea, in the area between the jungle and the sea, sitting in a tree of delicate, fanlike proportions. The bird, in my mind, was a particular reddish gold, with a yellow beak and blue markings on its chest. Its song was an outlandish, inconsolable squeal; years later, when I first heard John Coltrane and Archie Shepp, I recognized in them the sound I'd imagined.

On my first day at school my father told me that no matter what else happened, always be sure to share.

It makes life easier, is what he said.

We were attending a market where things were laid on tables and blankets. Bev and I in the early morning. Men and women had stationed themselves behind their pitch and were looking hopeful. The dim streets were crowded with enterprise. Here were plates, pans, toys, tools; all the makings of life. One sold only rope and string, another sold only rags. Most sold a little of everything. The most hopeful, the poorest, the most desperate, sold the unsellable; a single boot, a rusty fork, cracked cups, corroded batteries, bottles of half consumed alcohol. As we walked we pointed; occasionally we kneeled and examined something worth examining.

Bev was the most vocal, constantly asking, will you look at that?

She nodded at a pyramid of champagne glasses, stacked to a great height, in white boxes that said Bedford Wedding Supplies; mostly, here and there, chipped. A man peeked out and said, twenty pee a glass.

The thing that drew our interest, that stopped us, was that someone had written on one of the boxes, in a thick black marker: The Monster Of God.

Did you, I asked, write that?

Weren't me, said the man. Was like that when I got em.

Well, well.

Nothing, the man said, to do with me.

As we moved away he shouted after us: you're not looking at a blasphemer when you look at me.

And then, incredibly, there was Fritz, a hundred paces up the street, hunched over a pile of papers. We watched him for a while, we in our drabbery, he in his finery. His coat, striped with dark green, curtaining around him. After a moment he turned, saw us and threw open his arms.

Family! he cried.

He closed in on us and we tried, mostly unsatisfactorily, to hug. We bent and patted.

Find anything? asked Bev.

Not a jot. Said Fritz. Not a sausage.

He stepped away and said, I come for the show.

The show helixed around us. Life, rent, gro-
ceries, clothes, phones, hats, lipstick, hammers.
House plants too and lamp shades. All fermenting.

Fritz stood beaming at the day.

Well, well. Said Bev.

I have, said Fritz, found one thing.

He dug into his pocket, pulled out a yellow
box of matches, and showed it to me. On the label
were the words Maiden Lane Matches. The writing
was red; in the corner was a single blue fleur de lis.
Six months later, on one of our infrequent trips to
Wales, he gave it to my father. I stood between them,
these two unequal pillars of my life, and watched
my father slowly turn it, inspecting its feel.

I remember these, he said. My mother used
to buy them.

He turned them over again, fingering the scratch
pad. He pushed the box open and prodded the few
remaining matches.

Maiden Lane, he said.

He placed them carefully in his suit jacket and
said, thank you Fritz.

I thought Fritz might cry.

Later that year the match box turned up in a
painting, alongside a shaving brush, both arranged
on a green table; the same painting that, fifteen
years later, I gave to Fritz.

Bev and I sit arm by arm, a plate of cucumber
slices on her lap. One for Bev, one for me, slowly

between our finger and thumb. A slice of cucumber, undressed, without a cracker, is a very nice thing. Perhaps just a sprinkle of pepper.

The impossible, says Poole, is what we must look to. The impossible must be our goal. The light to light our tunnel. For ten thousand years mankind has done the possible and look where it's gotten us. Stuck in this cul-de-sac of monotony. This dull stupefaction. Until we focus on the impossible we're doomed to be always drab. And when I say drab I mean selfish, murderous, mean spirited technobrats.

There were fourteen slices of cucumber, seven slices each. Now a drink of water, later tea. After that dinner.

Space, says Poole, isn't a void. It's not a hole. Don't make that mistake. Space is as full and crowded and as packed as New York or London. Bursting at the seams is what space is. But full of what? That's the question.

Poole stands and fills his portion of the afternoon. He swivels his head, pockets his hands and says, that's the damn question.

Yes, agrees Bev, I suppose it is. One of the questions anyway.

Full of that which isn't earthly. Says Poole. Full of the spinning molecules that make music, that make myth, that make non-existence possible. Space is full of life and death and potential and the law and it's raining down on us every minute.

We each look quickly around. I for one see

nothing new. Only the boat, the canal, the brown weathered fields.

It's my job, says Poole. What I'm supposed to do. Tell you these things.

He says this apologetically.

And we're thankful, says Bev.

She eats her last slice of cucumber. I lift mine off the plate and as it passes in front of the sun I can see tiny pale seeds and translucent whorls and dark flecks; all gone in one bite. I slip my foot out of my sandal and place the bare sole against Bev's left instep. This is how we sit for a while.

My project today, my secret project, is to watch the way swallow wings beat and then go rigid, how they dip and zip above the trees. Off soon to Africa, to spend the winter warmed and dried. To be watched by other old men, some with weak blood, sitting in the company of their friends and wives.

I'm also wondering about how it is that some people can do one thing and other people can't. Wondering if it's skill or luck or persistence or breeding. Wondering about talent and will and strength and timing. How some people have one thing and other people have something else. And about how sharing, when it happens, either works or doesn't.

I'm old, perhaps in a wrong way.

And about how, when all questions are abandoned, we sit around dozing.

I have a pain near my waist. On my left side. Just below my ribs. Above my trousers. I barely notice it any more. I comes and goes.

I have, with Bev, shared something.

Today, Friday, is our day to call Fritz. We'll find a phone booth somewhere, punch in the numbers and shout. Tell him that we're fine, that everything's OK, that we're neither sick nor in trouble. That, against all expectations, we're looking after ourselves. I may or may not say something about the weather. He'll tell me some little piece of London gossip, something that means nothing to me, and remind me that we can always, at any point, come back and live with him. He'll use the same phrase he always uses: one big happy family. Then we'll each say goodbye and that will be that. Done. There's a lock coming up in a couple hours that has, according to our maps, a phone box. Perhaps there. Perhaps not. We're learning how it is to not be in control of our lives; to be moving at a speed that gives the appearance of control but, in reality is a speed at which anything might happen.

Poole is telling us about his winters in Wales. About a network of barns and hippies and abandoned properties. What I do, he says, is I mooch around until I find the best situation.

The best situation seems to be measured in warmth, available food, and a choice of company in the evening.

I like, he says, to be occupied when the sun goes down.

His favourite occupation being talk. Both to and from.

He's telling us now about a connected series of caves in northern Italy that have secreted away in them amphibious mammals the size of small dogs.

What happened, he says, is that the Italian government stock piled thousands of tons of butter and cheese there during the second world war and then, after the war, forgot about it.

The butter and cheese, he says, was eaten by a local kind of newt. The newt, unaccustomed to the richness of the milk, began evolving into an entirely new species. A mammal with scales and vestigial gills.

Milk, says Poole, is meant to be consumed by a bovine calf; it's full of natural growth hormones and proteins that will insure the calf grows to an animal that weighs over a thousand pounds.

Stuff all those hormones into an animal the size of a toad and you got problems, says Poole.

I've seen them, he says. I've walked amongst them. They're remarkably docile. They're green and yellow and have little fin type feet. Give them another twenty years and they'll have hands.

Before the Italian dog newts he was telling us about a place where he stays in Wales, a place in the hills above Trefglwys, a community of hippies where, he says, they leave you alone and let you be what you wanna be.

There's a forest there, he says, that's peppered with old woodman's huts. I find an empty one and move in for a few weeks. It's nothing fancy but it's mine. Or at least I share it with the mice and bugs and whatever. I do some hibernating and some thinking and I live on whatever I can get from the hippies. It's not a bad way to spend the winter.

He shrugs his bulky shoulders and says, I've spent worse winters in a centrally heated flat in London.

I don't doubt it. I've been there; I've seen it, lived through it; it's not good. The streets in winter seem to be organized in cheap and endless ways; a closed and closeted tangle, wherein people hoard, guard, steal; involving themselves with the all consuming task of surviving February. I have no desire to return. I seem to have a meager supply of desire these days. My desires being the size and length of lunch. The desire to navigate this floating world from one lock to the next. To not make a total balls up of this new life.

Six months ago, when my ulcer was at its fiercest, I often coughed and shat blood. My desire then was to live long enough to survive London. Now it's all about the afternoon, the evening, the morning. I look no further ahead than a handful of hours. I'm a chastised man. Stomach pain yes, but less. No bleeding, no heaving horrors. Things, out here in the wide open, have shifted.

I leave Bev and Poole to their exercises; I crowd into a phone box and dial Fritz's number. He answers, as he always does, after the third ring. His voice full of all the things he is; expectant, wary, on guard; his hello formed of a line of Ls: hellllllllllllo.

It's me, I say.

You, he coos. A voice from the wilderness.

Not exactly, I say. A voice from Ellesmere.

A balm. He says.

I hear some indistinct rustling and he says, tell me everything.

Everything, I say, would take too long. I'll tell you where I am.

I look around and describe the late afternoon scene: a country pub, a recently turned field, a hedgerow, a tow path, a tree (oak), a sky full of heavy clouds.

Yes, yes, he says.

How are you?

I have news, he says.

He always has news. That he has no news would be news. I wait to hear the news.

I'm joining the literati, he says. Writing a book. Me, Fritz. At my age. A scribbler.

I wait for him to explain.

Let me explain, he says.

I imagine him in his Eames arm chair, in his

green satin smoking jacket, in his silk slippers, in his early evening finery.

I proposed and was accepted. He says.

Who, I wonder, can say no to Fritz? Who is possessed of that inner strength? The best I could ever do was to walk away saying nothing, leaving the words unsaid.

And that's not all, he says. The best part...

He sighs and says, you won't be angry will you?

Why should I be angry?

You wouldn't rain on Fritz's parade would you?

I consider hanging up. Fritz is a trial; a well dressed and often entertaining trial, but a trial nonetheless. I wait for a moment and say, just tell me what's happening.

What's happening, he says, is I'm writing a book about your father.

My father?

Rescuing him from oblivion. Or so I'm to believe. So my publisher insists.

I watch as a flock of starlings land in the furrowed field. The birds have barely touched down before they're off again, swirling pin pricks against the clouds.

Rescuing my father. I say.

Not at all sure that he needs rescuing, that any of us need rescuing. Let us all remain lost; lostness being our natural habitat, the habitat in which we do the least harm.

Reminding the world, says Fritz, of his

singleness. His greatness.

Well, well is all I can say.

Is that all you can say? he asks.

I didn't think anyone cared, I tell him. Or cared enough.

People, says Fritz, care about what they're told to care about. That's how culture works.

I look across the towpath at the canal and our boat. I can see the tops of Bev's and Poole's hands as they wave left and right. I can hear the murmur of Poole counting. I tell Fritz I'm pleased.

Fritz knows I'm not pleased. Fritz knows me. Fritz knows how delicate is the balance of my life. Fritz knows I'm neither a good son nor a good man. That I'm a tangle of craziness. That my ability to empathize has strict limits. He knows I'm neither proud nor happy about this. He tells me about a colleague who's been arrested for selling forged Kandinsky prints. I don't care. I can't concentrate. I'm thinking about my father's hands, his shoes, his midnight eyes. His terrible gentleness. I grunt. Our conversation doesn't end so much as lowers in volume and intensity. What can I say? What have I ever said? We hang up. I open the door and kick the dried, accumulated leaves outside.

Later, after dinner, after cello practice, with Poole napping under the table, I wave at the world and say, it'll stir things up.

Bev smiles and says, things?

I imagine countless, numberless, tedious things.

Complications.

Poor little Mouse, she says.

Which irritates me. Enough already with the poor, the little, the Mouse.

I tell her that he wants to come out to discuss it.

Come out?

Take a trip. Maybe Montgomery. Said he could meet us there.

Now Bev looks worried.

Fritz? Here? In the country?

I guess so.

You can't talk over the phone?

He wants to show me some pictures. He wants my blessing.

Bev throws up her hands and says, so you're giving blessings now?

I wonder what it means to be blessed.

Just so long, she says, as he knows we're not going back.

He knows.

Poole is doing his wheezing, a sound more at home in a wood, as if a wind is knotting and tearing between trees. He gulps, rolls over and is silent. Bev reaches over and takes my hand. Her eyes narrow.

Let him have it, she says.

I grip her hand and shake my head.

Him? It?

Fritz. His scribbling. Let him have his book.

I nod. The night settles. The water, all around, is silent.

12

We are all burning in time,
but each is consumed at his own speed.

So wrote Jack Gilbert.

M y father taught me how to be alone but not how to be lonely. I learned that on my own.

My father was an aggressively private man. His great fear, both as an artist and as a man, wasn't that he might be misunderstood, but that, one day, he might be understood. That he might be picked over and explained. As if he was a complicated but ultimately solvable math problem. *He* meant this; his paintings mean *that*. Done and dusted, no more ambivalence. There were times, growing up, or as a young married man, when I'd ask his opinion, ask him what he thought of a certain book or a news story or friend's hair cut. Invariably, after a muttered well, well, he would say the same thing: your guess is as good as mine.

As if any opinion of his wasn't worth wasting time on. As if, in putting forth an opinion, he was filling up an already hopelessly cluttered world. As if a guess was something less than noble and all guesses were the same. As if that's all we were, a species of guessers. And as if those guesses were all we had.

There was, during his lifetime, only one published interview. There were numerous articles but only once did he consent to speak on the record. In the late fifties a small magazine called Picture contacted him; my father invited the writer to spend an afternoon; the interview lasted twenty minutes. I didn't see the interview until years later. Fritz showed me a copy and said, this, this interview, right here, this is why I love your father.

I found a copy of the magazine and still carry it with me. If my father saw the world in terms of images, I see it in terms of words. The interview, for me, more closely captures my father's hesitancy, his gentleness, his abstracted bewilderment, than any portrait of him ever could.

I include some of it here:

Picture: Tell me, if you can, about the process of planning a picture.
Herbert Hillier: I have to let it be, the painting, what it is outside what I want it to be. Do you see? It's all a mystery. Mystery is essential.
Picture: What would you say is your primary concern?
Herbert Hillier: The struggle, I suppose, to break down complexity into simplicity. Removing the divisions between decoration and something finer, something bigger.

Picture: How would you like someone to react to your paintings?
Herbert Hillier: Your guess is as good as mine. I would hope my paintings might hold time; slow time; let a person get lost. Let them breathe and be present.
Picture: A conversation...
Herbert Hillier: No. Not at all. My paintings don't speak. My paintings don't talk. They're not about words. They're prewords or postwords. They're unworded. They're pictures and only pictures.
Picture: Do you spend a lot of time thinking about, say, a particular plate or cup before you paint them?
Herbert Hillier: No. I let them be what they are and I paint them. I arrange them yes, but I don't think they want me to be thinking about them all the time. I spend a lot of time looking. That's where I put in the hours. Sitting and looking and watching.
Picture: How long does a typical picture take to paint?
Herbert Hillier: A lifetime. How long does it take to be who you are? The paintings are my version of a life, of getting inside a life, of showing a life, and that takes a long time.
Picture: What does a cup and saucer mean?
Herbert Hillier: Something different every time I paint them.
Picture: Nietzsche said that one's truest feelings come out when one is separated from the thing one loves.

Herbert Hillier: Well, well. Perhaps. Yes. Certainly being separated from something focuses the mind. When you're free to be alone.

Picture: *What is it you share with your cups and plates and bowls?*

Herbert Hillier: History. A being in the world. A place. Light.

Picture: *Are you happy with your place in the world?*

Herbert Hillier: I'm not unhappy. Someone, after all, had to be Herbert Hillier. Something had to be a plate. We all had to live somewhere. It all had to happen and it did. It does. It continues. It's really nothing to do with me.

Picture: *Can you explain that?*

Herbert Hillier: There's a poem by William Blake that says: He who binds to himself a joy/Doth the winged life destroy/But he who kisses the joy as it flies/Lives in Eternity's sun rise.

Picture: *Do you read much poetry?*

Herbert Hillier: Very little. I read very little. I don't have the time.

Picture: *Do you see much new art? New paintings?*

Herbert Hillier: Almost nothing

Picture: *Do you miss having that contact with other painters?*

Herbert Hillier: Not at all.

Picture: *Is there anything you miss? Anything about your life you'd change?*

Herbert Hillier: I'd welcome more silence. Less

talk. Less interruptions.

Picture: Does that include me, this interview?

Herbert Hillier: That, I'm afraid, includes everything.

There were no women in my father's life after my mother. After *her*. He had no interest. Or he had no interest that made itself evident. Perhaps there were curtained desires; who knew? I never asked; I wouldn't have had the temerity.

The feeling persists.

As concerns temerity and shame and seperateness. As concerns not wanting to intrude into his life. As concerns boundaries and walls.

And now there's Fritz and his bloody book.

I've never seen a photograph of my mother. When she left, all her pictures were destroyed. My father's reasoning was that if she no longer wanted to be here, then that decision was to be first respected and then extended; not only to her flesh and blood but to her image.

As I've said, with my father the image, the picture, came first.

I attempted, as a young man, to write a novel. A version of my life. It came, as have so many things, to nothing. I accumulated pages and pages of a lifeless scrawl. Eventually I burned it. I never told Bev. It was my own private failure.

I had tried to write about a lucky boy who had a gentle father; a father who told him: be as little like me as possible. Be as little like most men as possible. Be as much like yourself as you can. Most men are dull and without the necessary subtleties to make life bearable. They can't tolerate small beauty. Nor can they tolerate silence or weakness.

I wrote about how the boy took a trip and saw some things. How his body changed. How everything that occurred was both terrible and bearable. How sometimes he felt better. How he felt his relationship to nearly everything was slanted. And how a voice travelled with him, a voice hesitant and wetted and timid, that told him, I've never known how to talk to you.

Nor me to you. The young man answered.

The blooming and the glow, the dust, all the awkward parts, the blots and droppings, it all went on and on.

13

*There's no larger mistake possible than
to believe that an absence is a nothingness.*

So wrote John Berger.

There were times when I felt ostracized and imperiled, in my own private Elba, sitting behind my counter at McPherson's. We would argue about some small thing, some forgotten fine point, something of no importance to either of us, and off she'd go to Wales, where they'd spend the weekend drinking Darjeeling tea and listening to all that dismal pianoing. Lutes too and viola da gambas. Thomas Tallis and Purcell and William Byrd, John Dowland and Thomas Morley, all the love sick wanderers. All that God inspired purity. God knows what my father and Bev talked about. I never asked.

They may have found me, on occasion, mediocre and gloomy; yet I was more nearly in the world than either of them. I had one foot tentatively in the commercial realm. I met and dealt with the public. I looked, I saw, I listened, I noted. Perhaps it was my limited participation in the world that bound them against me. My jazz. My cheap fiction. My ice cream for lunch. My afternoons with Ric. My nights out with Fritz.

There was a book I read then that concerned a planet called Vendix, a planet made entirely of a substance called Twox. Twox was an unstable materiel that, given its peculiar chemical makeup, was prone to sudden and catastrophic collapse. But it was all they had, and from it they built their houses, their cities, their cars, their clothes, their lives. The material was described as having the rigidity and core strength of dried grass; it bent and twisted and was susceptible to high winds and water. Scientists had developed methods of refining and strengthening it, but it remained volatile. They lived, therefore, in a state of perpetual upheaval. There was no wealth because nothing lasted. Twox was the great leveler. Everyone had the same because what good did it do to have vast amounts of something that was worthless? Vendix lived in a state of benign collapse until travelers from Earth arrived with technology that turned Twox into something solid and stable. From this new vantage point of permanence the people of Vendix began building bigger and grander homes, vast cities, faster cars, reservoirs and storage facilities; they covered the planet with roads and fences and walls and towns. They experienced, for the first time, the accumulation of wealth. They grew greedy and restless, they were consumed with desires, they turned Vendix into a cheap and tawdry outpost of Earth. The novel ended with a group of scientists discussing the progress they'd made, the innovations that had improved people's lives, the solidity and strength they'd achieved, the exciting discoveries that lay ahead.

I remember going once, with Ric, in search of a man named Setzer. Ric had appeared at the shop in the late afternoon while Sun Ra and his Arkestra were in full flow, chanting about sleeping beauties and satellites; the day was damp and lackluster; I had no customers.

I got to go find Setzer, said Ric.

Setzer?

Setzer, said Ric, is a treat. Setzer is a legend.

He raised his eyebrows and said, it'll be a laugh.

I wondered if I struck him as someone in need of a laugh or someone who enjoyed a laugh. I wasn't, and had never been, an easy laugher.

Setzer, he said, is an education.

I must have looked skeptical; education, in my experience, rarely being a laugh.

Setzer, it turned out, was only three streets away, in the first place Ric thought to look.

You never know, he said, we might get lucky.

We did. We were told that Setzer was on the second floor, the second floor said the third; the third said the roof. Up we went, two further flights, and pushed open a door. There, between pigeon leavings and windblown bits, a man was sitting in an aluminum folding chair with a cat on his lap.

Ric, he said, rolling the R.

Ric smiled and Setzer said, you've brought a friend.

I wondered: so we're friends now? Ric and I?

Me too, said Setzer.

He held up the sleeping cat and said, meet Larry.

Ric nodded, glanced at me and introduced us.

Three men of the world at their leisure, said Setzer. And this guy.

He stroked Larry and smiled. We stood in the grey, besmogged afternoon. Below us cars and buses nosed along, tooting and growling. The streets were dotted with dazed shoppers. There were, I thought, 6 million of us metropolitans, each one unknown and at odds with the next, each one inebriated by noise and desire and arrogance, six million people who needed to be fed, housed and entertained. Six million citizens filling their terminal lives.

Larry, said Setzer, has a bad stomach. Don't you fella?

He gently rubbed the cat's belly.

Ate some bad fish didn't you?

Larry purred while Setzer smiled at Ric.

You, he said, have been a very lucky boy.

Have I?

You cleaned me out. Completely emptied the coffers.

Ric looked at me, smiled and said, stick with me son.

Setzer waved him away.

Get over yourself, he said. You got lucky. It happens. It was a flook and flooks happen.

He then launched into a long story concerning Ric's luck, a story that concerned a bet that Ric had placed on the dogs at Hackney Wick. The bet was a foolish one, a long shot, something called an accumulator; certain dogs had to win in a certain order over a certain number of races. They all came in.

As if, Setzer said, they'd all gotten together that morning, had a friendly chat and decided to make Ric a very rich and happy man.

He stroked Larry between the ears and whispered, you feeling any better?

Larry didn't answer. He rolled over and closed his eyes. Setzer mumbled something about fish and chips.

You wanna stay out of the trash my friend, he whispered and then looked at Ric.

I wondered if he was talking to Ric or Larry.

Ric had invested £50. He had made nearly £8,000. More than I would make in a year at McPherson's. Ric accepted his good fortune with grace. He gave Setzer a grand for 'services rendered', he gave me five hundred pounds for 'being a stand up guy', and gave Larry a hundred pounds for 'nothing'. He gave everyone on the third floor ten pounds each, left a pile of bills on the second floor, and took me out to a meal on Old Compton Street. He distributed notes to the waiters, the busboys and the cooks; he ordered champagne all around.

Ric, as I've said, was an entertainment.

The last thing he said to me that night, as we waited for a cab (Ric's treat), looking bleary eyed and swell, was, who the hell would ever choose to live outside the city? Eh? What kind of fool makes that mistake?

We arrive in Montgomery at mid-day, the afternoon being heavy and humid. Bev leans on the rudder and gentles us alongside the canal. Poole steps onto the tow path and loops a rope around a metal pole. He helps me down and for the first few seconds on solid ground I quiver, the earth seems to be slightly shivering. Light comes feathering through the willow and birch trees. The day, without brakes, rushes forward. There is, ahead of us, a church, a pub, a fist of houses and a tearoom. As we walk across the church yard we see Fritz, in his finery, sitting at an umbrellaed table. There's something dislocating about seeing him here, removed from the capitol, as if we'd walked not across a rural churchyard but across Regent's Park. The first thing he says, as he turns and sees us, is, good people!

He's bedecked (there's no other word for it) in bright summer garb; a blue and white striped shirt, a silk cravat, a cream linen suit. A straw hat above, pink and orange trainers below.

He opens his arms and says, bless you!

Two magpies are making noise beneath a yew tree. A squirrel high-tails it across the path. There are touches, here and there, of yellow. Bees too and butterflies. The whole thing is a picture of which Fritz would never approve. I can hear him say: sentimental pastoralism.

Bev introduces Poole and Fritz says, any friend of yours is a friend of mine.

We sit and Poole, looking heavenward, says something about the house of Aquarius, the moon of Jupiter, the rising sign of Virgo.

Poole, says Bev, is a hitchhiker.

Ah, says Fritz. A traveler. A man of the road.

Of no fixed abode, says Poole.

We talk for a while about nothing, the weather, the village scene, the miles Fritz has travelled and what he's seen, the train, the cab he'd taken from the station. Fritz, pleased by the shape and weight of Poole's unexpected presence, tells stories about his London doings; art openings and who he's seen there, articles he's read, a French movie that had bored him, an expensive but disappointing bottle of wine, a dinner he'd attended in Dulwich.

All of it, he says, empty without you.

He includes Bev and me with a quick wave and says, why is it always the best people who leave?

London, he says, is swollen with everyone you would, in a perfect world, avoid.

Poole smiles and says, motion.

Fritz squints at Poole and says, motion?

Motion, says Poole, or the lack thereof. People need motion to be the best versions of themselves. A static population is a dull population. Londoners, in my experience, increasingly, are a stagnant people.

Then he says something about celestial travel and ancestral journeys, about trekking from planet to planet, about how the British canal system mirrors the ancient routes from Sun to Moon to Earth. Fritz is mesmerized. He looks at me and smiles. Beneath the table his foot nudges mine. As Poole talks about intergalactic visitations Fritz makes a noise that can only be described as purring.

Ooh, he says, tell me more.

Poole does. Bev and I send each other signals. (C'mon, she says. I *know*, I tell her.) We wait while Fritz and Poole discuss a twelfth century astronomer monk, Articus VeMere, who spent ten years trying to prove that birds were travelers from a distant planet. When the pope finally decreed, in no uncertain terms, that all creatures on earth were the product of God's design, VeMere left the church, saying, there is no possibility that the same hand that created that ugly, clumsy and brutish being Man, could have created birds.

The Bishop Of Lyon, says Poole, a ninth century cleric, said animals couldn't go to heaven because they didn't contribute to the church.

VeMere, says Fritz, was imprisoned and stoned to death.

While birds, says Poole, flew around him singing.

No doubt, says Fritz.

When the church bell chimes three times Fritz turns to me and says the one thing I don't want to hear.

I have an open ticket.

Meaning he can stay as long as he's welcome.

Could I beg a bed for the night? he asks. We can discuss your father's book over dinner and I'll clear out in the morning.

He pats my hand and says, it'll be like old times.

I wonder to what old times he's referring; never have I spent the night in his flat nor he in mine. I look at Bev and she heaves a sigh that says, OK, just for one night.

You'll have to sleep on the deck, I tell him. There's a bench that pulls out into a bed.

Beneath the stars, says Fritz. Perfect.

Poole, I say, sleeps beneath the table. You'll be at opposite ends of the boat.

Pilgrims together, says Fritz. A happy band.

I'm thinking: pilgrims? A happy band? Us? An old man with stomach ailments, a woman whom he has consistently disappointed, a former bus driver and a London gent...

Fritz pays for our tea and off we stroll, the day built of layer upon layer of light, birdsong, refracting water, the smell of decaying leaves. We walk slowly, as if unwilling to leave solid ground. We board the boat and set ourselves adrift.

The burden of living is to be all ages at once, to be

buffeted by memory. I sit in the still dusk listening to Bev, Poole and Fritz; they're gathered around the table discussing some bit of arcana. I'm napping and not napping, one hand on the rudder, remembering a book I once read about a planet that suffered a hail storm of intergalactic quasars. The storm was so severe that it interfered with the planet's molecular workings. Suddenly everyone's intelligence was drastically reduced; they were, over night, a race of imbeciles. No longer could they perform even the simplest of acts; cars and clocks and wells and lights were all left to rot. No one could understand how a toaster worked. What the hell was electricity? How did an engine operate? The civilization they had carefully constructed fell apart. The population was reduced by three quarters. The world returned to a state of undeveloped wilderness. The people learned simple acts of self survival. They lived in small wandering groups. The world, in every way, was a better, healthier, happier place.

And I remember a jazz record I once owned that had a quote from the I Ching by Lao Tzu printed on the back cover:
Small countries with few people are best.
Give them all of the things they want,
and they will see that they do not need them.
Let the people value their lives and not migrate far.
Teach them that death is a serious thing.
Even though they have plenty
of horses, wagons and boats,

they won't feel the need to use them.
Let people enjoy simple technologies,
let them enjoy their food,
make their own clothes,
be content with their own homes.

14

The cost of flight is landing.

So wrote Jim Harrison.

We are, I think, drifting south; we could be anywhere. The dark brings its own map. Bev is gathering dinner; Fritz pours wine. Poole is entertaining them with tales of winters past. I hear him say something about living in a rich man's shed while the owner was sunning himself in Spain.

I stayed there for a month, says Poole, drinking his sherry and bathing in his Koi pond.

Poole, expanding, lounging on the bench, pushes and pulls at the air. His hands claim the night; he points at a far hill and says, two years ago I spent three months in a sauna.

Three months?

The main house was empty, locked up tight. Someone's second home. Out back there was an unlocked sauna. Stack of wood a mile high. I had a lovely winter. Bought bags of potatoes and roasted them in the stove. Laid around naked all day. Lost twenty pounds.

In the darkness I can barely make him out. He's just more night. I can see his eyes and, now and then, his teeth. He's laughing now, talking about how it's impossible that he's fifty-seven.

Not likely, he says.

His hands swoop around and he says, earth years go by so quickly. Twenty minutes ago I was eighteen. This morning I was thirty.

His head bobs up and down and he says, you're telling me I've spent fifty-seven years on this planet?

Bev brings in a plate of something and puts it on the table. It smells green.

It's all screwy, says Poole.

Fiasco, says Fritz.

Shit, says Poole. I know for a definite fact that I've spent some time floating around the galaxy. Ten, twelve, fifteen years.

I can't see his face exactly but I'm sure he looks indignant.

Time, says Fritz, is relative. Time is a slippery partner.

Bev brings another dish and says, that's it. That's all there is. It'll have to do.

Smells divine, says Fritz.

Pasta with stuff, says Bev.

Just what I fancied, says Poole.

Earlier, looking at a crumpled map, Fritz had asked if we could drop him off in Berriew; I'll spend the night, he said, then disappear like the dew.

He's been carrying around a small portfolio, eight by twelve inches, covered in marbled paper. It now sits at his right elbow. He raises his glass and says, to cohorts.

Poole raises his glass and says, to time, to space, to gentle trespasses, to the unseen visitations of past lives.

Oooooohhhh yes, coos Fritz.

Food is passed around, plates are filled. As Mr. Salter said, life is meals. We busy ourselves, candles flicker, the night is nearly warm. My stomach and its attendant troubles have been mostly quiet. I don't eat much. I listen to an owl do it's hooting. Bev eats quickly, leaves her plate and opens her cello case. She tightens her bow, scratches out a scale and begins playing. Poole and Fritz are talking about several things at once; foot paths in Wiltshire, the abundance of Chinese businessmen in London, ash trees in Brecon, the poetry of Rolf Jacobsen. Fritz spreads his hands and says, my cup runneth over.

I wonder how big the cup is, what the liquid is, what kind of cup it is, where the liquid is going and who's going to clean it up.

Bev is playing something I recognize, Chopin or Ravel or Debussy or one of those French fellas. Long fluid dips and slides. It fits inside the night. I remember once sitting with my father on a bench over looking a small valley when he said, I feel sorry for anyone who paints. Anyone who paints seriously. They sit looking at a perfectly beautiful landscape and all the time, instead of enjoying it, they're thinking, how can I rearrange this and order it and make it better on my canvas?

I let Poole and Fritz carry on talking while I

clear the plates, wash them in the canal and make tea. Peppermint with a slice of lemon and a plate of ginger biscuits. I bring the pot and cups to the table. There's something, I can feel it, happening between Poole and Fritz. A fascination, a twinning, a meeting of two mythical brutes. I pour the tea and Fritz clears his throat.

I have, he says, something for you to look at.

He taps the portfolio and gives me a look that says, surprise!

He knows how much I dislike surprises. I sit back and cross my arms.

Don't look so moody, he tells me.

My stomach, suddenly, burns.

It's nothing terrible, he says.

He pushes the portfolio to me and says, open it.

I don't want to. What good has ever come from poking around in another man's portfolio?

Go on, says Fritz.

The portfolio is tied with green velvet ribbon.

It won't bite, he says.

I listen to Bev swoop from high to low to thin and quavery. I can just about make out her fingers as they skip across the strings. I untie the ribbon and move closer to the candle. Inside are several pieces of paper, what appears to be four or five portraits and a letter. The portraits are of a young woman; in one she's holding a cat, in another she's reading a book, in a third she's sitting, hands folded, in the dusk. She wears a simple green dress. A further picture is of all the portraits together, hung on a gallery wall. The letter is from Thompson Brothers Gallery, Cork Street, London. I quickly scan the letter; it's addressed to Fritz and signed by Gerald Thompson. There are only a few lines:

Dear Fritz Hughes,
Please find enclosed four photos of the paint-ings we discussed. According to our records the paintings were exhibited for three weeks in November 1929. They were then removed from public display at the artist's request and returned to the artist in January 1930. We have no further information. If the paintings weren't among Mr. Hilliers personal effects at the time of his death we can only assume that they were sold privately or destroyed.
Fond Regards,
Gerald Thompson

Bev is winding down, playing a series of descending scales, each one quieter and slower than the last. Finally silence.

The only portraits your father ever painted, says Fritz.

He reaches across the table and places his hand on mine. I nod and pick up the photos. The light is weak; I look at her briefly; her pale eyes and unbending lips, her clasped hands, the uncertain curl of her hair. There's something, around the mouth, that's familiar.

I tell Fritz, these aren't for your book.

He nods.

I lift them together and, with a single act, rip them in half and then in half again. Fritz says nothing. I stand, walk into the kitchen, open the rubbish bin and toss the pieces in, amongst the coffee grounds and lemon rinds, the tea bags and potato skins. I can hear Bev packing away her cello. On the kitchen counter are two cups, a plate and a fork. One cup is pale yellow, the other white. The plate is decorated with grey flowers. The fork has a wooden handle. The arrangement is uncannily like one of my father's paintings. I stand in the dim light and see my father's hands gentling saucers and ladles into position, an inch to the left, half an inch closer together; I feel his fingers on my arm, pointing out a fallen leaf, or a pleasing tea pot in a charity shop. His hands always promised me something. I can hear him say, well, well; I can smell the turpentine and oil paint on him. He would, I think, like it here, floating around like this, mostly cut off from the fierce thrust of things. I stand for a moment more, letting my weak blood gather around my waist.

When I return to the table Bev is discussing sleeping arrangements.

Poole, she says, is under the table. Fritz, you'll be up front on the bench. We've got a couple extra blankets.

To be among family is comfort enough, he says.

It's the kind of thing Fritz says. He talks in excesses. It's the way he lives; high and careless and fragrant.

We sit for another half an hour, too lazy and tea drugged to move, listening to Fritz's plans for my father's book.

My life's work, he calls it. The story I was born to tell.

Finally Bev makes a decisive move away from the table; the last cups and plates are cleared; Poole loudly runs through his nightly breathing exercises, honking and blowing. I bring Fritz his blankets and an extra pillow; the owl calls.

In the night I'm roused by the sound of footsteps on the deck. Bev is already awake.

What's up? I ask.

No idea, she whispers. They've been moving around up there for a while.

I sigh and close my eyes. There's no way I'm going back to sleep now. I push at my pillow and regret giving one to Fritz. I'm a two pillow man. I wiggle around; the night is filled with the enemies of sleep. Bev bends in close, smelling of soap and something sour. She drapes her arm over me and asks if I remember Southwold.

Southwold?

Yes.

Of course.

A Suffolk holiday forty years ago. The plan was

to rent bikes in Aldeburgh and cycle to Cromer, in Norfolk. We made it as far as Southwold, eighteen miles, one day's journey, and decided to stay there the entire week. We rented a beachside chalet and walked along the beach, collecting sea kale and samphire.

Waters Edge, says Bev.

I nod. The name of the chalet.

Two pounds for a week.

I nod. Above us a chair is being dragged across the floor, followed by a burst of whispered conversation.

And Herbert?

Yes, I remember Herbert.

A feral seaside cat that appeared each morning and evening. We named him after my father as the resemblance was undeniable. We would breakfast together, Bev, Herbert and I, Herbert sipping from a plate of milk. He shared with my father an instinctual politeness, an unwillingness to intrude, a ghostlike calm. His eyes too were similar, a reluctance to look at you straight on, an unfathomably private agenda. We discussed taking him with us when we left but couldn't bear to separate him from the sea.

I like it here, she says.

Here?

Wherever we are.

Me too.

I picture two things simultaneously. Miles of

terminal canal water, choked with sluggish frogs and abandoned shopping trolleys; and the antiquated blood in my stomach, doing its weary best to heal the unhealable.

Mouse?

Yes?

She gives me a kiss.

No sounds from above. Only water lapping, Bev breathing. Quiet.

...old bachelor hungry bird, aging-hungry-man-
bird, and how I hate desire, how I need pleasure,
how I adore love, how difficult middle age is!

So wrote Glenway Wescott.

In the morning we're alone. I say the words slowly: we're alone. I repeat them. I say them louder. I think of Mandelstam writing: to be alone is to be alive. I find Bev in the kitchen and tell her.

We're alone, I say.

She looks up from her bowl and says, I know.

The day promises rain. A few dark spots have already appeared. There's a wind doing things in the trees. I say it again, just to hear myself say it.

We're alone.

Yes.

Bev smiles up at me.

Have they gone for a walk?

More smiling.

Is that it?

Fritz left a note. She says.

A note?

On the table.

She points past me. I turn and she follows. The promise of rain hasn't come to much, only dull skies and a low breeze. I walk the length of the boat and find, on the table, anchored beneath a stone, a piece of paper. I can make out, even from this distance, Fritz's grand scrawl. I turn to Bev.

Have you read it?

She shakes her head as if offended.

Only the first line. I was waiting for you.

Light is ribboning, here and there, between the clouds. I'm in no hurry to read it. I'm in no hurry to do anything. Hurrying is something I did long ago. In a hurry now only to be left alone. I look across the canal the church spire, silver now in a strip of light.

I'll have my tea first, I tell Bev.

Whatever it is, it'll be worse on an empty stomach. I pat my defective gut. I'm only allowed peppermint tea now. It settles me.

C'mon, I tell Bev. I'll make you some coffee.

She takes my hand and we return to the kitchen. I ask her if she heard anything else last night.

Not a peep. Only this morning. Around six. I heard them leave the boat. Thought they were going for a walk.

I boil water, prepare my pot and Bev's cafetiere. We take our cups back to the table. The church bells ring once; eight thirty. For thirty years I woke each morning at eight, left our flat at eight forty-five, bought a croissant on Old Compton Street and made tea at the shop. In the summer I cycled; in the winter I took the tube. I waited on customers, played my records, read my books, saw who I saw. In the evenings, most evenings, we ate dinner, made tea, listened to the radio, read, and played backgammon. Lives change. Bev leans back, lifts her chin and closes her eyes, as if offering her face to the sun. There's no sun. I reach over and pull Fritz's note out from under the stone. The first sentence, written in larger script than the rest of the note, says: *Dearest Conspirators We're Off.*

I read it aloud to Bev and she says, go on.

I continue, reading slowly, sounding like a weak copy of Fritz.

I've retreated to the city and taken Poole with me. He has advised that we should start early and so we shall. We'll call a cab from the village phone box, the man who dropped me here said I could call anytime, night or day.

Don't think me greedy for relieving you of Poole. It was a moment of mutual recognition. I'm ready, he said, for some city doings. I've offered my services and he's accepted. He'll stay with me until such time as he sees fit.

It was in the face of your father's paintings that I was first made aware that grace without quietude is mere posturing. I continue, in the company of yourself and Beverly, to learn that lesson.

You remember, cher ami, ten years ago, when we went out for an evening of grown up culture, starting at an exhibition of Anne

Redpath paintings and ending at Ronnie Scott's
listening to Archie Shepp? Miraculous night.
An evening against which all others are measured. The Redpath paintings were jewel canvasses of flowers, chairs, ornate wallpaper; the
Shepp concert was a lesson in flight, in history,
in process, in theology. Do you remember the
awful wine at the exhibition, the slightly better
wine at Ronnie's, and the gorgeous bottle of 54
Armailhac sauvignon at mine?

And do you remember, that night, I showed
you a little painting I'd bought by Bill Traylor, a
painting all in blue, of a man reading a book? It
was, and is, very dear to me, and expensive, and
when you looked at it you said, oh, my father
would have liked this.

It was the same thought I'd had when the
painting came up for auction.

How often have I used your father's approval
as a marker?

Cher compagnon –

I want to be a man, even at my age, of which
people might say: he may yet achieve something.

I will do my best for your father; the book
will, inevitably, be as much about myself as
it will be about him. Such is the treachery of
biography.

Poole is flailing about doing exercises. He
intrigues me. More than that, he excites me. I'm
of an age when excitements are rare and must be

grasped!
  Departure –
  Au revoir –
I miss you both already, vastly, I must see you
soon!
  Fritzy

How quickly one thing becomes something else,
what's past is forgotten, routines are resumed, habits reclaimed.

We haven't moved. The boat is moored and
tethered.

There's only us.

We've eaten, napped, talked; the weather has
messed around, birds have gathered in the ash
trees, leaves have scattered; we've sipped tea, read,
cooked. Now Bev is playing. Life is this.

Can I tell you about a day I once spent with my
father? Do you mind? Let me tell you this before
I go. I was, at the time, a newly married man,
worried that Bev was too good for me, that I was
unsuited to married life, that even in the midst of
new pleasures ruin was inevitable. It's a feeling that
persists to this day. Back then, when much about
my life was unexpected, I saw less of my father than
I should have. I was weak minded and interested
only in those things that made my life easier.

The week before my father's birthday I called
and asked if Bev and I could spend the night.

Well, well, he said. Of course.

We arrived in the early afternoon. My father met us at the station and we walked to his house on the edge of town. As we walked he talked with Bev about her students, about a recording of Schubert's Wintereise he'd bought, about concerts she'd been to. My father was as he always was; hesitant, interested, vague, equivocal. He had tea waiting for us, Darjeeling and scones. He showed us his most recent canvasses; he pointed out which ones were, to him, successes and which were failures. He dismissed one painting of a bowl and gravy boat; the bowl, he said, was feeble, the colours were impossible, the light was without weight. He shook his head pityingly as if discussing the work of an overindulged child. We had an early dinner (lentil and parsnip stew with dumplings) and played Scrabble. I gave him a box of chocolates and a bottle of wine for his birthday; Bev gave him a recording of Chopin's nocturnes.

In the morning, he said, we'll go for a walk.

He had never before volunteered to take us anywhere; I was intrigued.

A walk?

He made a gesture that could have meant anything.

A place, he said, that I go.

The night was finished. We did the innumerable small little things you do preparing for bed. Unusually for me, I slept well. In the morning, after a quick breakfast, he led us to the bus stop.

Any minute now, he mumbled.

Wearing what he always wore; tweeds and wool and here and there leather patches. When the bus came the driver said, morning Mr. Hillier. Same as usual?

Yes please, my father said and off we went.

Nothing was said during the ride. We watched the day. There were sheep in it, everywhere, and rock barns and dark birds and trees just barely big enough to be called trees. There was no one else on the bus. After half an hour we got off and followed a bridle path across an open field. On the far side we crossed a small bridge and entered a wood. Fifteen minutes later we found ourselves standing next to a wooden fence. From the way my father stood, and from the looks of a small patch of worn earth, this was it. This was where he'd brought us. This was our destination. We looked out across a wind slapped meadow of sea grass and burdock and comfrey and hogweed. A single hazel tree stood next to a holly bush. There was sun light out there doing things; behind us the woods were dark. The hazel was moss green and then lighter, then lighter still; the sun rested and faded. And was then bright. The tall grass kneeled this way and that, all of one motion. The sky swam. There were other things out there, things unseen and unheard, things furred and winged and hard shelled. It was a world unspeakable, unquantifiable; dull and wet and alive. We stood for twenty minutes; I knew enough to say nothing. Finally we returned through the woods and to the bus stop. As the bus appeared and slowed my father turned to us and smiled. He seemed to apologize.

I come once a week. He said.

Routine, order, chance, manysidedness, impermanence, loss, separateness.

We rode back in silence.

Bev burrows into me, her legs warm against mine, her arm across my stomach. My damned stomach. Ripped and tattered. My stomach that says please, I'm hurting, I'm weary, I'm in need of tenderness. It's three in the morning. The boat trembles. Bev breathes deeply and easily. Do things repair? Do they get better? Does that happen? At this age? I listen to an owl doing owly business.

Bev lifts her chin. Her breath warms my ear.

Mouse, she says.

Yes?

Her lips brush against my cheek.

We must be careful.

Careful?

You know...

I know.

My hand finds hers; I grip it. There is night.

ACKNOWLEDGEMENTS

I woud like to thank the following people:
Cathy Knapp and all at MWA,
Mid Wales Arts Centre (midwalesarts.org.uk);
Nick Hand and all at The Letterpress Collective;
Caught By The River (caughtbytheriver.net);
Rob Ryan, Jerry DeCicca,
the Phillips clan… Clovis, Tim and Tora;
Tony Smith, Thayer Nichols,
Mary Kornblum, Bill Henderson,
and Loraine Morley.

ABOUT THE AUTHOR

Jeb Loy Nichols was raised in
Missouri and Texas. At seven-
teen he received a scholarship
to art school and moved to
New York City. From there he
followed friends to London.

Jeb now lives off the grid in
mid-Wales where he writes,
produces art, makes music,
and plants trees.